The Blue-Eyed
B

David McQueen

Published by
Four Oaks Publications
4 Oaks Road, Shiplake,
Henley-on-Thames, Oxon RG9 3JH

ISBN 0 9518155 0 4

Typesetting and make up by
T & S Typesetting, Willow House,
Battleborough Lane, Brent Knoll,
Somerset
and printed by
Antony Rowe Ltd, Chippenham, Wilts

Contents

Illustrations by Janet Duncan

Note: All characters in this book are entirely fictitious.

BY THE SAME AUTHOR:

Hods and Sods

DEDICATION

To the chaps on the jobs

Preface

FEW men are so drawn together and interdependent as building trade workers. Whether on the scaffold or seated round the stove in the site mess shed, they communicate endlessly on every subject under the sun, sometimes even resuming argument or discussion when relaxing with pipe and pint during the evening visit to their local.

Pickstock, a typical small, English town has, over the years, supported a complement of builders commensurate with its size, only the occasional business failure or aspiring tyro — often a graduate from the ranks — ruffling the ingrained composure of the established mastermen.

By a natural process not yet fully understood, there emerges from within the town's environs just sufficient skilled and unskilled labour to fit the bill at any given time and, even when an outside firm muscles in, it is usually a temporary phenomenon because wily old Parkinson goes into reverse until the building employment ratio per thousand of the population conforms to the enigmatic formula.

Other forces, too, combine to present a united front, for local builders defend habitats like blackbirds guard territories — intent on driving off interlopers, especially those of their own kind with take-over ambitions, using every practical and pricing device to thwart and harry.

Most mastermen peak in their late fifties, at which time, often pressured by their wives, they will pick a plot of ground in a prime residential area and build themselves a house against the onset of retirement. Until then many will have lived in an apartment over the office with yard alongside, the better to administer the business and keep an eye on the comings and goings of men and materials.

The interplay of relationships between master and man, foreman and clerk of works, architect and client, and the blending of knowledge, skill, procedure, attitude and reaction, generally produces not only the desired result, but stimulates the property owner to a consuming interest in the one nationwide industry whose yards and functions are familiar to everyone.

'Give us a price. . .', or 'what would it cost. . . ?' or, 'Can you do me a wee job. . . ?' are commonplace introductions between client and builder, rough sketches and spot quotes giving way to architectural drawings and contractual arrangements as the work involved increases in size or complexity.

Ultimately, however, it is the man on the job who turns plan into reality, craftsman and labourer who, with their special skills, create the three-dimensional object the customer wants.

At the yard, the carpenters shop is the focal point, the place where, given half a chance, the site man lingers to chew the rag after appraisal of the finished article or discussion about the construction of some purpose-made piece of joinery.

On site, it is the mess hut with its combustion stove and leaky corrugated iron cladding which serves as clubroom and snuggery, the forum where the man with the gift of the gab is accorded the highest acclaim just so long as he sustains relevance and wit in his spiel. And if he be labourer or mechanic, or merely improver, then so much the better for democracy.

Here, it is not always the best educated, the man of standing or the craftsman who makes the grade; many a budding Bevin has won his spurs in the rough and tumble of the mess shed during a spate of inclement weather when there was nothing in the dry for the gang, and back in the office the boss sat at his desk feeling sorry for himself.

So, if you pass by a building site in Pickstock on a wet and windy day when clouds scud wraithlike across the sky, you can be pretty sure that the reeking stovepipe sticking through the roof of yon battered old shed signals another council of barrack room lawyers, bird fanciers and political theorists in session.

Humbugs and Acid Drops

RESENTMENT, like unrequited love, niggles, and tends to keep a man in suspense and out of humour, sometimes resulting in reactionary measures entirely out of character.

Take the case of Wally Jones, a man slow to anger, generally well-liked and, until prodded and pushed by Betsy, his wife, quite satisfied with things as they were and happy to ply his trade as a leading bricklayer just so long as he had his pint and could watch a football match every Saturday afternoon in season. The flashpoint came one Sunday when they were sitting by the fire in the front room of their council house, tucking into tea and ham sandwiches.

The wife, sharp-nebbed, astute and fed-up with the daily grind, urged him to have a go on his own. One of these women who was forever changing the furniture around, it occurred to her that it would be feasible and interesting to tinker similarly with her man's means of livelihood.

"You're the best bricklayer in the district. You know as much about building as anybody; more than some. Sam Lappitt hasn't even got a trade! You've nothing to lose. I've three hundred quid you can have to help set you up — my mother says we might as well have it *before*, than *after* she's dead — and I'll keep your books for nothing for the first twelve months."

He knew it was no good protesting his ignorance. In fact, years later, he realised it was only his ignorance that kept him going, for if he'd had an inkling beforehand of some of the situations he'd get himself into, he would never have taken it on.

In the beginning, it was certainly a hard grind.

Lappitt and Thomson, builders long established and thus comfortably ensconced in their respective businesses, watched with curiosity, recalling their own first faltering steps; especially Thomson, in whose employ Wally had spent his first ten years in the trade. But the brickie, once launched, stuck at it and very soon had half a dozen hands, a concrete mixer, a secondhand truck, enough scaffolding for a pair of houses, more work than he could comfortably manage, and a thumping overdraft that would have frightened the life out of him, given the time to think about it.

It was the overdraft that started the trouble because, eighteen months after it had been arranged, the sympathetic, soft-hearted, encouraging bank manager — "a lovely fella", Wally had told the wife at the time — was transferred to another branch, and the man who took his place, as knowledgeable and thorough as his predecessor had been easy-going and risk-taking, applied the screw, warning that the overdraft limit was due shortly for reconsideration and, meanwhile, he would be looking for a substantial rundown in the use of the bank's resources.

Wally was flabbergasted. He was just getting into his stride. Penchant and relish for running his own show fuelled his every action; ideas for expansion had been hard to rein. Now, here was this new chap at the bank acting like a cold douche, clouding the future with his negative, sober-sided, lacklustre projections.

The wife's mother died and left a cottage into which they moved from the council house. It had a third of an acre of scrub land at the side which, when cleared, proved useful for containing builders' tackle, and although the manager suggested that the deeds be put on charge at the bank, they had misgivings on discovering that this would make no difference to their borrowing powers, would in fact, at best, only serve to prop up their slim collateral. It was the first time he'd had a bank account, never mind an overdraft, and he found the whole business puzzling.

There was no difficulty in getting hold of the work, and carrying out the jobs efficiently to the clients' satisfaction was child's play compared with the frustration and anxiety of handling the finance and keeping on top of the paper work.

Despite his enthusiasm, there were times when he wished he was back on the trowel wondering what Betsy had got for dinner, or whether Pickstock United really had the players capable of taking them into the third round of the Amateur Cup.

For her part, although she had never done this kind of work before (in her single days she had been records clerk and general factotum in a drapery business in the town), Betsy soon got the knack of costing up the jobs, carefully recording the man-hours involved in the various operations, and breaking down the figures into feet super and cube, yards, rods and the rest, for future reference.

Instead of wasting their time watching the telly in the evenings, as they had done previously, they would settle down with *Building Practise*, or *How to Estimate*, books borrowed from the library, sometimes even teasing out technical problems hitherto beyond Wally's ken.

Not only that, Betsy kept tabs on the details of the estimates sent out, building up an exact knowledge that buttressed her man's backwardness when asking the price for the job. So, naturally enough, when a solicitor's advice was sought on the registration of W. Jones (Pickstock) Ltd., it was recommended that she should have a seat on the board.

It was about the time of the changeover of bank managers that Wally contracted to do the Tomkins job.

This was a double garage and workshop with flat over, under a pitched roof, to be built at the end of a long garden, with access to the rear, and sited so that screened by an orchard it was out of sight of the house, some hundred yards or so distant.

Without too much argy-bargy, he got quite a fair price for the job, but after receiving a couple of hundred pounds for starters, found Tomkins reluctant to part with any more.

Several times he applied for interim payments, only to be put off on some pretext or other and, by the time the timber was delivered for joists and roof, Wally decided to suspend operations. He had become more than concerned and was certainly resentful of the client's attitude towards him. Tomkins, an incomer whose business was "in the city", had that easy facility for making Wally think he was asking for the earth, when all he was after was his due rights under the contract. Wally likened him to those well-to-do gents who kept their tailors waiting for years for their bills to be paid, easily handling the bespoke men who were over the moon, bowing and scraping, when given a mere fraction of what was owing to them.

Eventually, he got a cheque somewhat short of what it should have been, but when it bounced at the bank, he raced hot foot to the Tomkins place and gave him a piece of his mind. The client, after a mild apology for the inconvenience caused, passed the matter off airily as an "arithmetical hiccup" in his accounts and informed him that the matter would be put right forthwith. Notwithstanding this, it was ten days before the replacement cheque was forthcoming and when, once again, it came back marked "refer to drawer", Wally went wild. Again, he repaired with all speed to the Tomkins house.

It was Mrs Tomkins who came to the door.

"Hello, Wally!" she greeted enthusiastically, as

though delighted to see him, and with a disarming smile cocked her head to enquire his business. She was a pretty woman, years younger than her husband who, it appeared, was not at home.

If he did not know it before, Wally knew now that he had got himself a very slippery customer indeed; and one with a woman to match. He realised that the very ease with which Tomkins had dealt with the first bouncer should have told him that here was an adept performer in the art of negotiating financial tightropes; a man of no conscience, on the make at other people's expense.

"I'm afraid I know nothing of my husband's business affairs," she replied artlessly to Wally's enquiry. "You'll just have to wait until you see him yourself and take it up with him. He's gone abroad." She smiled sweetly.

Far from weakening under her spell, resentment mounted at being taken for a fool. He sniffed her expensive perfume and bristled.

Raising her eyebrows, she encouraged innocently, while he stood transfixed:

"But he'll be back — possibly in about three weeks' time." Again she turned on the sugary smile.

Standing on the doorstep shaking with rage, Wally uttered a queer, demented cry, a cross between a bricklayer in torment and a man without a roof to his mouth.

Encouraged by the then bank manager, Wally early on had begun negotiating the purchase of Pickstock Hall, a large Georgian house of some slight architectural significance, which had been empty for years (in the war it had been used by one of the Ministries for storing an assortment of software — gas masks, bedding and the like), and had been up for sale for as long as anyone could remember. Everybody in town who was somebody had looked at it at one time or another, with the idea of development or demolition, or with some more fanciful scheme in mind, but when it came to the nitty gritty, each and every one shied off.

As the years passed, the asking price plummeted, to the extent that it was not difficult to deduce that snags abounded. Wally, left to his own resources, would never have thought of being seriously interested in acquiring the house — more a mansion than a house, really — but in those first, halcyon days, sponsored by the bank and spurred on by the drive to multiply, everything seemed possible.

Encouraged by the nice bank manager, he made his decision and went in with both feet.

Very soon he was padding around the house in the late evenings weighing it all up inside and out and bursting with ideas. He had bought it for a song and, in the beginning, really got his money's worth, looking around, prodding, scraping, digging, prising up floorboards and calculating the value of the timber carcasing, the lead on the roofs, the beautiful handmade bricks and so on. It stood in about an acre of ground, hemmed in by terraced property which, in pre-planning days, had been allowed to nibble away at its environs.

No sooner did it get about that he was going to pull it down, than he ran straight into trouble. He found he would need planning consent to demolish, then, when the word got around that he really had bought the property, all sorts of people who wouldn't have stumped up a brass farthing to save it, suddenly became interested in the preservation of the old pile, even stopping Wally in the street and threatening to have the law on him should he remove one brick or tile.

He had letters from the Georgian Society, the local and county authorities, architects, surveyors; also all manner of well-intentioned and not-so-well intentioned people telephoned to enquire whether there would be bricks for sale, or how much did he want for the fireplaces, and was he going to build flats or maisonettes in the grounds?

He found he had disturbed a veritable hornet's nest, yet so far he hadn't done a thing except complete the purchase. He hadn't even made application for demolition.

Mind you, in the first month or two after he bought, he found great satisfaction in possession. Except for an odd half hour or so in the evenings he had no time to spare during the week, but on Sundays he would take Betsy along to walk around the mansion, point out the magnificent W.C.s with flower pattern designs inside the pans, explain the intricacies of making the ornate cornice moulds and generally admire the Georgian workmanship and flair. In a rare, spontaneous display of excitement, they even had a cuddle and held hands in the little private closets adjoining the main drawing rooms, giggling like a pair of kids when Wally minced and preened in imitation of a Regency buck.

It was a fantastic feeling to look out of an upstairs window down to the elaborate ballustrading of the grandiose, upswept double stone staircase ascending from the end of the drive to merge at the main entrance to the house, and to think that, at least for the time being, they were the sole proprietors.

However, as the weeks became months, Wally got more than anxious as to what he was really going to do with the house, especially when the planning officer confirmed that he hadn't a hope in hell of obtaining consent for demolition, adding that the Ministry boys were no doubt waiting in the wings ready to pounce and obstruct whatever was proposed.

The new bank manager had been asking some pertinent questions too. He had pointed out that the increased facilities arranged by his predecessor, to cover the purchase, would have only very short-term sanction as far as he was concerned.

Then, one pay-day morning, when he went to the bank to collect the wages, the counter clerk told him that before presenting the cheque, he was to see the manager.

Wally's heart missed a beat and, as he waited apprehensively outside the manager's door, he fumbled in his trouser pocket and produced a small paper bag.

He was never without an acid drop or fruit pastille, for, before seeing the bank manager, clerk of works, or other superior or awkward customers, he would pop a sweet into his mouth. It made him feel and appear much more relaxed and pleasant, taking the edge off his nervousness, the taste seeming to counteract apprehension as to the outcome of the palaver. When he had to open his mouth he would slip the sweet under his tongue and no-one would be any the wiser.

It was a ploy picked up from his dad, a commercial traveller who, in his early days, whenever he had to attend an interview prior to a change of employment — a frequent occurrence — would, on the pretext of feeling light-headed, call at a chemists for an on-the-spot nip of *sal volatilé* which, by soothing his dry mouth and putting him at his ease, produced the *persona grata* impression that sales managers rated even higher than experience or qualification. Later, he graduated to acid drops, which he found did the trick just as well.

The manager of the bank, determined to impress his authority on the builder, kept him waiting, so much so that Wally, sucking his second sweet, lapsed into reverie, recollecting the times when he fell out with Betsy, especially when they were not on speaking terms for a day or two. It was then, becoming tired of the sulks and wishing to bring about a thaw in the situation, she would prepare an extra special dinner. As a rule it worked wonders. Again, it was purely a question of taste, the chemical reaction of pleasure in the mouth causing a resurgence of well-being which ousted pessimism or depression and kidded the grey matter that, not only was all well, but that a bright new era was about to dawn.

"I've called you in, Mr Jones," explained the manager when at last he beckoned Wally into his office, "because my accountant tells me you're over your limit and, with today's wages added, the figure agreed would be considerably exceeded."

He waited for a response, but Wally contented himself by swapping the acid drop from one side of his mouth to the other.

"It is necessary, nay, imperative, that we discuss the future conduct of your account. You must appreciate that, under no circumstances, must you exceed the limit agreed."

Again, Wally's reaction was to shovel the acid drop around his mouth, reasoning that the man had made a statement, not asked a question, though he was puzzled by the phraseology, for he had no reason to believe that his account was any less well-behaved than the next man's.

"I don't think I'm getting through to you, Mr Jones."

Wally slipped the acid drop under his tongue. "The only reason I'm over the top is this job I've got. The customer, Tomkins, owes a big amount. He's gone abroad."

"I can't help that. You're overdrawn. It's up to you to rectify the position."

"The last manager said he'd always see me okay; give me leeway of a few hundred in emergencies — so long as it was never more than a thousand."

"Did he! Well, you might as well know right now that it is not my policy to work that way. A limit is a limit and

I must ask that you work within the agreed figure in future. Is that understood?"

"Okay," Wally conceded, scowling his displeasure; hurt because, he reflected, if it hadn't been for Tomkins, this situation would never have arisen. It made his blood boil to think about it.

He got ready to leave.

The manager looked down his nose at him. "I'm not finished yet. What about this job you mentioned? Tomkins? I'm given to understand you've taken the law into your own hands? Hardly conducive to successful business expansion, I'd say!"

"Oh, ah?"

Judging that he was going to get no further on this tack — Wally not being in the informative mood — the manager, adopting a fractionally more conciliatory tone, indicated the papers on his desk:

"To regularise the position, I've drawn up this undertaking. At the moment the only collateral we have against your borrowing is a life insurance policy and the deeds of Pickstock Hall. If, for the time being, we are to continue on the same basis as hitherto, I shall require you and your wife to sign these papers, which include taking your cottage on charge. And I shall, of course, require the deeds to be deposited at the bank."

Wally gulped, and what was left of the acid drop promptly slid down his gullet.

"So, what you're really saying is that we sign these papers, or else? No wages?"

After hesitating a moment, the manager assented.

"If you like to put it that way, yes. You must appreciate that I have to look after my bank's interests."

Incensed, Wally stood up, and bravado took over.

"And I'm telling you, I have to look after my interests. The answer's 'No', and you can go to hell!"

He stalked out of the office and, as he passed the

counter, informed the staff loudly and luridly what he thought of their manager.

He would have been quite willing to let the bank have the deeds of the cottage, Betsy and he having already come to the conclusion that, if it would ease the pressure, they would deposit them. But not now. The man got his goat. Hackles up, he now had no intention of agreeing to anything, for it seemed that every time he had been to the bank lately, this man had been yapping at his heels.

Shaking his fist at the bank, he clambered into his truck, through the open window shouting to the passersby, "The man's a bleedin' twister — a pompous twit — a bloody humbug!" Shoppers, sensing a disturbance, looked nervously, anxiously, at the receding vehicle.

By the time he turned into the car park at the *Drovers* a mile up the road, he had simmered down and concluded that this time he had well and truly burnt his boats. On the credit side, he knew Betsy had put aside seventy pounds from her mother's bequest for emergencies, and he did have the deeds of one tiny plot of ground, but. . . .

As he drained his pint, he thought to himself: "What in hell's name am I going to use for wages? Betsy will beat the livin' daylights out of me for this."

At precisely the time Wally was in unilateral conference at the *Drovers*, Lappitt and Thomson were meeting for a business drink at the *Nag's Head*, a house they both used on occasion around lunchtime. After some discussion on the pricing of a job for which each had been invited to tender, Lappitt, eager to update information on what he considered "the latest Wally indiscretion", turned to Thomson.

"You've heard about his garage job, of course."

"Who hasn't?"

"The man must be ravin' mad!"

"Oh, I don't know. What builder hasn't been tempted to do just that? Haven't you?"

"Yes, well, but. . . ." Lappitt supped his ale, then returned to the point.

"But fancy actually pulling down your own work, carting it all off, leaving the site clean as a whistle! And what I can't understand is how he could shift all that brick rubble in his little truck?"

Thomson puffed reflectively at his pipe.

"He didn't. I lent him my lorry."

"You what!"

"Yes. I knew he couldn't, or wouldn't, hire. I happened to meet him in the *Cherry Tree*. He told me all about it — what he was going to do. I had a lot of sympathy for his point of view."

"So you did him a good turn?"

"Sort of. Mind you, there was a nice lot of hardcore — came in very handy for that out-of-level council job I've got at the Pump Lane school."

"Ah! I see."

"Pity it hadn't been lime mortar so's he could've re-used the bricks."

"I hear he left the oversite?"

Slowly, Thomson commented.

"In his frame of mind he would have dug up the lot — foundations and oversite. I thought it was more trouble than it was worth, and besides . . . ah, well, never mind, we won't go into that."

"Must be a tough customer this Tomkins. I'd like to see his face when he gets back home. I remember having a job like that once; couldn't get a brass farthing out of the man until I stopped him and his wife in the street one day — locals, they were — and told them that any time I saw either of them out and about I'd shout the odds so's everybody would know. I knew the woman wouldn't stand for that. Got my money the next day."

Thomson grinned appreciatively. "There you are, then! Wally calculated he wasn't going to get paid at all because, being incomers, they didn't give a damn. I thought that was very perceptive of him. Got his head screwed on has Wally. Might make a go of it yet."

"And what about this Pickstock Hall he's bought? Bloody fool! Bitten off more than he can chew there, I'd say." Thomson sighed. "Had a look at it myself once when timber rationing was on. Made enquiries about pulling it down, but there was nothing doing. He *could* get well and truly clobbered."

Switching the subject, Sam said, "E's got 'old of one or two 'andy chaps, ain't 'e?"

"Whealer wouldn't like losing Dud Chapman for one. When you've worked with a man you've no need to ask what sort he is, and Wally, being a good worker himself, knows the score."

"And what about Dingo? Perpetual motion, I'd say."

Lappitt was always interested in Thomson's opinion, and on the odd occasion when they met up with one another would use him as a sounding board for whatever was in his mind at the time.

"Rough bricklayer, Dingo, but what a worker!" responded Thomson. "Years ago, when he worked for me, his little gang was the only one to show a profit in the bad times. 'Course, he wasn't all sweetness and light — wanted handling — but he didn't talk much and got on with it."

Sam reflected, "What I can never understand is why chaps like Dingo spend all their spare time in the betting shops and pubs, specially the labourers. You'd think they'd 'ave learned by now that you never get anywhere that way; 's commonsense."

"Get away with you! Since when has common sense

had anything to do with it — too stodgy a diet for them. They want to be encouraged, talked at, excited, inflamed. It's no good telling the likes of Dingo that 'common sense will prevail' when he knows bloody well that it won't. He wants a bit of excitement in life, *now*! — takes to drink to encourage his fantasies, so long as the money lasts, and so would you if you had the background of Dingo and others like him. . . . Of course, it's a hell of a come down when he wakes up to the old treadmill, but at least he's had a respite."

Using his glass as a pointer, Thomson declaimed, "Look at us standing here at this time of day! Between these four walls, there's not a jot of difference between them and us, only a microscopic bit of control; which doesn't necessarily make us any better, only different. Wally's a case in point."

He emptied his glass.

"Anyway, this won't pay the wages . . . I'm off."

In the main it is the minor things that come to mind in distinguishing one man from another, idiosyncracies we pigeon-hole and trot out whenever a particular person is talked about or recollected.

This is especially so in the case of those of us — the great majority — whose plain, commonplace features pass inconspicuously in the crowd; people like Russell Taggart who, content enough with his ordinariness, nevertheless was widely known as Taggart the Tie, and, although coming from a nail-biting family, was the odd man out in possessing beautiful and well-manicured hands which, when interviewing clients, he was apt to display clasped on the desk in front of him.

Years before, when he joined his firm as a junior solicitor, he had been quickly shoved in at the deep end to take over the court work which his seniors were eager to relinquish in order to concentrate on more lucrative and seemly employment, leaving the Tie to serve and foster acquaintance with the seamy side, and so to acquire, over the years, character judgement not generally to be noted in conveyancers, last-will-and-testament men, and similar deskbound types.

As a young man and tie fancier, he had been known to spend his last few bob on a sudden whim; and the beautifully formed Windsor and half-Windsor knots which were his delight and pride, were the envy of all who clapped eyes on them. He collected ties by the dozen — plain, striped, woollen and the rest — hundreds of them hung in serried ranks within wardrobes and closets, others stuffed into drawers in almost every room in the house. By the time he was thirty and married, his mania had reached epidemic proportions.

"Why don't you let me give some of your old ones to the scouts for jumble," his wife would plead periodically, knowing full well that he'd have none of it; although she did thank her lucky stars for his addiction when Christmas and birthdays came round.

It takes a crisis to squeeze out the best in a man, whether it be talent or judgment, and after a couple of drinks had cooled his temper, Wally was convinced that his next move was with Taggart the Tie.

The solicitor laughed explosively when he heard what lately had taken place at the bank, encouraging Wally to go into the minutest detail not only in regard to his interview with the manager, but also his dealings with Tomkins, and the subsequent demolition job. (With regard to the latter, it came out that because the firm had so much work in hand, he had done the brickwork himself, which was just as well, for he would have had to think twice about taking liberties with another man's bricklaying by reducing it to rubble: Dingo, for one, would no doubt, as a matter of principle, have demanded his cards.)

Fingering a nice new, royal blue silk tie, Taggart said, "So the upshot is that you're minus the week's wages?"

Tentatively, Wally responded, "Yes. I wondered if you would consider lending me something — on a temporary basis, of course. I have this bit of ground at Piggot's Bottom. It's not much — fifty foot frontage — but I thought you might set it off against a loan?"

"Where's the deeds?"

Wally produced an envelope of estate proportions and handed it over.

The solicitor, after cursory examination of the deeds, laughed noisily and slid the envelope and documents back across the desk. He growled, "I'm not a bloody pawnbroker, you know."

Wally, squirming, slumped back in the chair, watching the well-groomed hands and the light from a side window glancing off the glossy silk tie. His spirits were exceedingly low, and surreptitiously he slipped an acid drop into his mouth.

Taggart adjusted his hands on the desk and looked keenly across at the builder.

"You've got yourself into a rare old mess. However, I'm glad you had the sense to come to me because I had a visitor earlier on this morning: one, John Timson Tomkins, no less!"

"He's back!" Wally, eyes popping and with more than a trace of anxiety, enquired, 'What's he want?"

"He wanted advice on the criminal prosecution of W. Jones (Pickstock) Ltd, for demolishing his property."

"Bloody hell."

"Yes, you might well say so. You could be charged with maliciously causing criminal damage. What d'ye say to that?"

Wally, hackles rising, exploded, "'E ain't paid for it, so how could it be his property?"

"A good point. But, tell me, how exactly did you leave the site? Did you make a clean job of it?"

"Cleared it all away, 'cept the foundations and oversite."

"How much have you had from him to date?"

"Just two hundred quid."

"And would you value the foundations and oversite in excess of that figure?"

"Definitely, worse luck."

"So we could establish part ownership, eh? — argue that all you have done is to demolish that part of the work that still belonged to you?"

"No doubt about it."

"I see!" murmured the solicitor speculatively. He rose and took down a book from one of the shelves ranged behind his desk, then, after thumbing through one or two other hefty tomes, spoke softly to himself.

"Yes, yes, we have a precedent. Fear not the slings and arrows, Wally. Justice giveth every man his own." He sat down again.

"Incidentally, I let Tomkins tell me his side of the story before I enquired the name of the builder. Eventually, I had to tell him that you were my client and so couldn't act for him. He was not very pleased — stormed out in a huff. Seems from what you say, I ought to be thankful for that."

Taggart pressed a button on the desk and in came a smart lady secretary.

"Give me your wages cheque, Wally. Susan! I want you to draw a cheque for this amount on our No. 3 account; you'll find the breakdown on the back of Mr Jones' cheque. Take it over to our bank and bring me the money.

"Now, Wally, when Susan returns you slip off and pay your wages. Then, soon as you can, come back and I'll have a note ready listing all the information I want from you — *facts and figures*, Wally — works in progress, what's owing to suppliers and sub-contractors, sales invoices, debits and credits, collateral — the whole shooting match. I'll set it all down as to how it is to be done.

"*Then*, armed with these facts and figures that you're going to dig out, *mine* from your records over the weekend (Betsy'd better be on her toes!), you will come here first thing Monday morning, and you and I will go across the road and see *my* bank manager. A change of banks is indicated, don't you think? What say? Will that suit you? I wouldn't do this for any old builder, y'know."

The next week proved hectic for Wally, but after the dust had settled, and reverting to habit, Betsy and he took stock in their cottage parlour on the Sunday afternoon, ham sandwiches and tea laid out on the side table.

"No doubt about it, Betsy, there are some genuine people around. Look what The Tie has done for us, and without security! And Thomson! If it hadn't been for his help that Tomkins job would have bin awful difficult — after walking out on him the way I did I couldn't really have complained if he had given me the cold shoulder. But he always did treat me fair, did Thomson. It just shows, you don't really know a man till there's a hoo-ha. Come Christmas, we'll have to present the pair of them with a few bottles in appreciation of their help."

Betsy's point of view differed slightly.

"Oh, I don't know. Thomson got paid in brick rubble, and that solicitor's not as soft as you think. He knew he was on to a cert *and* that he'll get everything back with interest."

And the Georgian property?

"Beginner's luck," was how Lappitt put it when he heard it had been resold to a local couple who came in for a bit of money when the wife's father — Elson, the butcher — died before his time. Their dream it was to live in just such a mansion. Not everybody's cup of tea, of course, but they made a go of it, and when the planners did a U-turn (as they often do if you can wait long enough), they hit the jackpot with a permit for a row of half a dozen retirement bungalows in the grounds, the balance of land ceded to the council for an open space.

Not so many years after their crisis, Betsy could look back well satisfied with the result of her goading that first Sunday afternoon in their council house parlour. Now, she had money to burn — or so her friends and acquaintances declared — and was proud of her part in the build-up of W. Jones (Pickstock) Ltd.

Wally, too, was pleased with himself. He gave up the acid drop habit as confidence mounted and peptic ulcers threatened; his stomach, he claimed, was his best friend for whenever he hit the bottle, or overdid the grub stakes, it served immediate notice that it was not to be trifled with. He found an abundance of fulfilment as a masterman and, although still partial to a pint of best bitter, sampled the upstairs life with a bottle of wine on the table at Sunday dinner.

As vice-president of Pickstock United, he now sat in the best seats which, after all, was only proper, since it was he who built and partly donated the new stand in thankful memory of the many happy Saturday afternoons he had spent standing on the touchline.

Ripe for Development

THE prescribed sustenance to keep her alive was a trickle of dried milk in boiled water, with a shot of morphine to steady the pain that racked her whole body from time to time. Yet, strangely, she appeared to be in the pink of condition, eyes alert and sparkling, skin fresh and blooming.

Alternately, Millie looked from her sick bed out of the window across the cow studded pasture beyond the cabbage patch, then refocussed on a print tacked to the bedroom wall; it was captioned *Babes in the Wood*, a sepia-tinted, old-fashioned print depicting Victorian children playing at the foot of a great oak tree and, often, she used it to transport herself back fantastically to her own childhood in the halcyon days before the Kaiser's war.

Rosy cheeked and pillow propped, she sported a flimsy nylon nightdress with a primrose coloured bed jacket drawn loosely about her shoulders.

To Mary, her neighbour, come to see if there was any chore that wanted doing, she explained:

"Of course, I'll never set foot out of this room again, and I didn't need the doctor to tell me. The hospital said I have a rare liver complaint; it's cancer, really, cancer of the blood. But I've seen to it that Jack is provided for. I've put everything to rights and I'm quite easy in my mind."

She smiled contentedly.

It was all so humdrum, so completely controlled; no tears, no emotion, no dramatics: Millie, sensible old lady that she was, having put her house in order now quietly awaited whatever was in store beyond the pale.

She had no religion, though surely someone somewhere had passed on this remarkable composure, enabling her to face finality with steadfast resolve.

Mary, a pleasant, handsome woman nudging middle-age — she had lost her electrician husband when he became too familiar with a high voltage cable at the paper mill where he worked — marvelled at her neighbour's courage in coping with so desperate a condition, and said so.

"Nonsense!" Millie asserted. "We all have the constitution and capability we were born with. It's bred in us. I don't believe you can alter anything if it's in your make-up; at least, not a lot."

With as much show of affection as she was capable of, she continued, "I want to thank you, Mary, for all you've done for Jack and me these last few months," then, without changing her tone, "In case I don't see you again, I'll say goodbye now. . . ."

With more than a generation gap to contend with, Mary found it difficult to look Millie in the eye, even though she had become infected with her matter-of-factness and was afraid that, recognising this, it might cross the old lady's mind that she was callous. A thin wisp of grey hair straggled down Millie's cheek to the corner of her mouth, and the younger woman restrained herself from stroking it back into place, afraid this might be too great an intimacy.

She had been sitting on a small, straight-backed bedroom chair, but rose now and went to the side window from where, poking above the tops of the cherry trees, she could see the gable-end of her own two-up, two-down end of terrace cottage.

"The cherries will soon be ripe," she said. It was the first thing that came into her head.

She knew she should have kissed the old lady, but all emotion between them was stilled, and anyway a natural backwardness had taken over. She leaned across the bed, patted the primrose bed jacket inadequately and, mumbling a hurried goodbye, left the room.

If Jack had any material ambition in him at all, he certainly realised it when he was left the superbly situated old cottage with the cherry orchard, backing as it did on to green belt and built as it was at the best end of the little country town. For some unknown reason, the cottage had been completely ignored by the developers' scouts who periodically combed the district for potential building sites, winkling out property suitable for conversion, and chivvying neighbours into selling back gardens that hadn't seen a spade since the coming of television. As far as Chalky Lane was concerned, it was as if the real estate fraternity had contracted a blind spot.

When the cherries ripened, his friends were only too willing to help compete with blackbird and starling in stripping the trees, and although some of them carried away much of the fruit for their own consumption, Jack would just smile benignly and tell them to come again. He was quite satisfied with the present arrangements, for, in a good year, he would pick up as much as ninety pounds from the local greengrocers; "bunce", he called it, which hitherto Millie and he had shared equally between them, most being devoted to extra comforts for the home or, sometimes, gardening aids and implements.

A carpenter by trade, he was an easy-going bachelor, a gentle giant whose humanity was his most attractive feature. Here was a man worth calling a man who, on a fine summer evening sitting alone under the trees, would lightly finger a penny whistle, not just for his own amusement but, when in full peep, to the delight of all who walked by on their way to the *Graveldiggers Arms* at the foot of the lane.

. . . with his penny whistle in full peep

Sometimes his friends called him an old softie, especially when, exasperated by the depredations of the verminous grey squirrels which haunted the little orchard, he resorted to his catch 'em-alive rat traps, only to turn the little devils loose again when caught; practically apologising for his evil intentions!

The only time he crossed swords with any man was when the cherries needed picking and he took time off work to harvest the main crop; a habit of longstanding this, for during all his years as Millie's lodger, he had painstakingly looked after the orchard and vegetable patch.

Even before her demise, Millie had made over the cottage to him, affirming her dearest wish that it should continue to provide shelter and home for the only man she had ever cared tuppence about.

Jack's boss, Sam Lappitt, a small dumpling of a man never seen in public without his rumpled porkpie hat — it protected and at the same time diverted attention from a prominent, glossy bald pate — invariably got hot under the collar at absenteeism, especially since the firm had taken on an architect designed house whose specification bristled with purpose-made joinery, the production of which depended heavily on the carpenter's special skills.

So, the evening visit to the cottage came as no surprise to Jack. And Lappitt lost no time in coming to the point.

"Surely it wouldn't hurt to give us a couple of days in the shop and at least finish off them bull's-eye winders. It 'ud put the bricklayers on, and I'd be ever so grateful."

The statement was a rare mixture of cajolery, threat and plea.

"You know I always have time off for the cherries!" Jack was mildly testy, for the pair of them went through the same rigmarole every year. It seemed inevitable that cherry picking time should coincide with the firm's most urgent business; but, of course, with architect and customer yapping at his heels, the builder's concern was understandable.

For many years there had existed a curious relationship between the two men, for Lappitt was in the habit of turning to Jack whenever he had a ticklish problem on hand. Faith in his judgment was implicit.

Often he would scramble up the well-worn steps leading from the yard to the carpenter's shop and, leaning against the timber rack, would plead, "What should I do, Jack?" or "What do you think, Jack?" or "We've got a rare problem here, Jack!" and then, without waiting for response, would give chapter and verse to his latest conundrum. On labour relations he was especially weak and sometimes became quite erotic in his anxiety to bridge the dialogue gap between master and man.

While the guv'nor gabbled away, Jack would suspend operations at the bench and, walking over to a dark corner at the end of the shop where his jacket hung on a six inch nail driven into the roof plate, would emerge twiddling a piece of fresh green parsley. Wherever he went he carried a few sprigs in his lapel, and was seldom seen in the street without a parsley stem sticking out of the side of his mouth. He deployed it as other men chewed the cud with matchstick, toothpick, straw or tobacco wad. It helped him concentrate, he said, and considered it a great aid to digestion. His addiction had started years before when Millie persuaded him to cut out the fags for the sake of his tubes.

The two men had been born and bred in Pickstock, went to school together and, later, drifted into a kind of non-profit-sharing partnership, Lappitt early on having to take over the family jobbing business when his father suffered a crippling confrontation with a brick lorry. He would have preferred a real partnership and, give him his due, had said so. But the carpenter was adamant; he was totally without executive or fiscal ambition and felt amply rewarded when his advice proved sound.

Sam Lappitt, though never able to fathom this kind of altruistic service, nevertheless found it vastly beneficial in the day-to-day running of his business, and decidedly profitable. True, he did hand over one or two bottles of spirits at Christmas time (Jack's inordinate pleasure on receipt of which giving the builder a momentary stab of humility), but, otherwise, the carpenter was quite content with a copper or two above the rate, and the holiday-with-pay stamps that went with the job.

In the space of twenty years the firm had been built up from a small jobbing concern to house building status with a sizeable turnover including contract and jobbing work.

"I hear the old girl left you the cottage, then?" Lappitt ventured as they made their way between the trees towards a rough old elm seat in the middle of the orchard. He had a knack of switching obliquely to another subject when it suited and, as the cherry juice leaked from the corner of his mouth under a droopy moustache, he studied Jack while waiting for a reply.

"Dear old Millie!" Jack intoned, almost emotionally. He had been extremely fond of his benefactress, with whom he had lodged for many years; she had looked after him like a mother.

Lappitt slipped a few more cherries into his mouth, expertly spitting out the stones as though this was his staple diet.

"Worth a fair bit of money and ripe for development," he surmised.

"What! that old cottage? Have you seen the roof spread? It's doin' the splits."

"Every penny of fifteen thousand."

"As much as that?" Jack looked flabbergasted.

"I must say I do like the look of them eyebrow dormers." Speculatively he glanced at Jack. "Any time you want to capitalise, you let me know. We could fix you up with a semi or a bungalow at the right price. You could do all your own carpentry and decorations, and pocket the rest. It'ud be a nice little nest egg for your old age."

"And the orchard, what about the orchard?"

"Worth nothing for building — mostly in green belt."

Of course, that was not at all what Jack had meant. But he couldn't help pointing out, "It goes right round the house on the west side."

"Yes, there is that. We might just squeeze in a single; it could put a few pounds on it."

He eyed the carpenter closely, half convinced that he might indeed be willing to sell.

"Tell you what I'll do, Jack," he suggested. "I'll give you sixteen thousand and shake hands on it now!" Thereupon, he flopped back on the seat as though overcome by his own recklessness.

"Ah, wait a minute, Sam! I never said I'd sell, did I? Anyway, what would I do with that kind of money?"

"What would you do with it? Why, you could invest it! put it in a building society and, instead of wearing yourself out cherry picking, you could take a Mediterranean cruise every year, or an African safari, or anything else you fancied. There's no limit to what you can do when you've got money!"

Jack's grunt expressed his disbelief and, although he kept mum, he was recalling how each year the guv'nor and his lady stayed at the same second-rate boarding house at Clacton — with all *their* money!

A dozen or so chickens scratched and grubbed about under the trees, and Lappitt, allowing his attention to wander, watched the boss hen reflectively as it strutted and clucked its weight about.

Helping himself to a few more cherries from an overhanging branch, he said to Jack, "Take your time and think about it," adding cautiously, "Mind you, I'd be the last to persuade you against your will."

Anxious to give the impression that he was quite at ease, he stretched himself, stood up, then, stooping, took off a shoe and hopped about on one leg while shaking out some imaginary grit. The shoe removal was an out-of-doors cover-up ritual perfected over the years to hide embarrassment, or done when he was stumped for something to say, or the altercation had reached an awkward turn.

It disconcerted anyone with whom he was talking and would put an opponent off his stroke; which, of course, was sometimes what was intended. Reaching down to re-do the shoelace gave him added time to decide his next move while the other fellow gaped uncertainly, thrown off balance by the unexpected performance.

Jack, of course, being used to it, didn't bat an eyelid, though he was aware that in this case it signalled a nervousness on the part of his boss, a condition which invariably preceded his coming to the point.

A cool breeze got up and the branches of the cherry trees threshed about, scattering the midges which were out in force. For a time neither spoke. Lappitt sat down again. Clearing his throat, he began.

"There's something I'd appreciate your advice on. . . ." Away from the yard it seemed politic to be rather more polite than usual, especially when about to pour out his troubles.

". . . .it's that young bugger, Tibby," he burst out savagely. "I'm having more bother with him. He's got completely out of hand since that tech carpentry teacher at the college told him he was in line for the Silver

Trowel. What d'ye think he's done now? He's gone and mucked the special kitchen unit you started him on, and he's practically ruined the piece of Afromosa we got for the fireplaces — twenty quid down the drain! And there's the Stoker affair . . . what d'ye think I should do about it, Jack?"

The carpenter had shown more than a flicker of interest, but before replying selected a fresh piece of parsley from the chromed holder fixed to the button-hole of his old sports jacket.

"Give 'im a clout on the ear'ole?" he suggested, flicking off the excess water before placing the parsley sprig in the corner of his mouth.

The latest series of Tibby incidents had started after the carpenter proposed that the apprentice be given site baptism to observe his reaction when exposed to the realities of life on the building. Jack had worked hard to implant in him the principles and mysteries of the trade, but, though willing enough and good at paperwork, there was a lot to be desired on the practical side, all the drumming and tutoring seeming to have little effect.

The management was apprehensive regarding his ability to survive as a fully fledged chippy when finally he left the protective enclave of the yard: so it had been decided to put him under the spec. site carpenter; a trial run for two days a week.

Tibby was delighted. Work in the open air suited him and he found the antics of the men engrossing.

For example, there was Stoker and his crony, Archie — an odd pair by any standards — in whom the apprentice boys took an absorbing interest. The two men had served together in the navy and, such was their affinity that, after completing their time, not only did they continue to find pleasure in each other's company but, flouting orthodox social sensibility, actually cemented their union by setting up house together.

They even job hunted in tandem and had been taken on by Lappitt when they offered their services as the nucleus of a navvy gang with drain laying experience. Naturally, it soon got about that they were, well, somewhat on the queer side, but this idea was confounded when, admittedly for a limited period, Archie went off with a neighbour's wife, and Stoker, not to be outdone, found a kind of solace in the arms of a sixth form high school girl, his junior by almost a generation.

However, when the gloss wore off, both men concluded there was no future in either link-up and, re-establishing their partnership, determined to maintain it in a better state of repair; although Stoker made such a deep impression on the high school girl that she pestered him for years, even after she married.

Thereafter, it would appear that both men signed the pledge of celibacy, and the extra-marital ambitions of some of the neighbourhood housewives roused by the unexpected shenanigans of the odd couple, soon abated.

It must have been the difference in make-up that brought them together because they were as chalk and cheese: Stoker, a Glaswegian with an inherent fondness for the bottle but, nevertheless, hard-working and reliable on site; Archie, mid-Bucks, mild-mannered, generally affable, though at work apt to depend overmuch on the Scotsman's muscle.

Archie, though displaying much more economic stability than Stoker, was noted for his subbing mania, the record of which, kept on foolscap sheets within the petty cash book at the office, had all the stamp of a bank overdraft account. The totals had been running for years, though the amount owed at any one time was seldom more than thirty pounds.

Like a rep or a professional man feeling vulnerable without a bank overdraft arrangement, Archie, when threatened with solvency, would hare down to the office to draw against the collateral of his next pay packet. He even took a certain amount of pride in letting his mates know when he had "a bit of business to transact with old eagle eye", the elderly sobersided Baptist who kept the books and costed out the jobs.

"Good god, Archie," Lappitt had been heard to exclaim, "if it wasn't for your subs we could cut the office staff in half."

Surprisingly, Archie looked after his money, which was just as well, for Stoker seemed forever "on the ear'ole". It was their main source of dispute and, at times, they bickered away worse than a married couple.

Stoker was lusty, rumbustuous, extroverted. Some men womanise, some spend their time money-making; Stoker's all-consuming interest was poaching. Since boyhood he had never been happier than when out and about, a favourite lurcher to heel, his eye on the lookout for someone else's pheasant, partridge, rabbit, duck or trout.

He was in the habit, from time to time, of raising the price of a pint by raffling his latest poach — a mallard duck perhaps, which he would transport sitting with its neck poking out of the basket on the front of the rickety old boneshaker of a bike he used for commuting between home and site. The fact that it was the same breed of wader known to frequent the stream running through the meadows at the back of the row of cottages where he lived had, of course, been generally recognised, but a nice, fat bird made a tasty meal and there was never a dearth of takers when Archie — he it was who held the purse strings — went the rounds with the roll of raffle tickets kept to hand for the purpose, believing as he did that the printed word lent a fine air of integrity to the proceedings.

Always the duck was presented live, for that way it

somehow seemed more valuable, and should the lucky winner be too squeamish to screw its neck, Stoker would oblige for a small fee; a couple of fags maybe, or a fill of tobacco.

One morning, during the week following Tibby's appearance on site, Stoker arrived with his latest captive. With the foreman's permission, he released it for the time being in the kitchen of a house waiting for the plasterer — a subcontractor currently giving Lappitt the run-around — then, carefully pocketing the back door key, he whistled his way over to the shed to load up the dumper with stoneware pipes and fittings.

He was not too bothered when, in the middle of the morning, a brickie pointing up a gable-end, drew attention to a duck wandering about the site.

"No' mine," assured Stoker confidently, nevertheless feeling in his trouser pocket for the key. "Why, yon yin's no hauf the size."

Certainly it was not altogether unusual for the odd duck to be seen in the vicinity, part of the site being low-lying and boggy, with Old Father Thames rolling along not far away.

However, suspicions were actively alerted when Stoker realised that it was a pinioned bird (he prided himself on never failing to take precautions), and confirmed when he caught sight of the unusual and distinctive albino patch above one of its primaries. Immediately he downed tools to investigate.

The back door of the house was locked right enough, the kitchen window secured and the temporary inside door battened-to. Yet, sure enough, the bird had vamoosed. He couldn't understand it. Looking extremely puzzled, he tipped his greasy cloth cap and scratched his head. No doubt about it, some devilry was afoot. (Although he had worked on the site from the start, he was unaware that the keys of many of the back door rimlocks were interchangeable, a fact that had quickly come to the notice of the observant Tibby.)

Yells of encouragement from the workers on and around the scaffolding followed Stoker's strenuous efforts at recapture, armed with a roll of hessian, while the apprentice boys were not only loudly vocal but, when the bird was eventually caught and reincarcerated, openly disparaging.

As a rule, the two indentured bricklayers were at least outwardly respectful to Stoker and Archie, neither of whom had any time for apprentices. Stoker, especially, would give them the odd boot or cuff whenever he felt like it. So it was fairly obvious it was the carpenter lad who was shoring them up, stiffening resistance to disciplinary tactics, and it was typical, and perhaps not too surprising, that after lunch Stoker went out of his way to drop a brickbat on Master Tibby's foot as the latter passed by a half-built manhole balancing a couple of lengths of seven-by-two on his shoulder.

"Clumsy me!" was the navvy's only concession to an agonised protest that he had done it on purpose.

"I'll tell Parsley on you," Tibby threatened weakly, rubbing a badly bruised instep. But Stoker only chuckled with satisfaction as, ripping open a new cement bag with the edge of his shovel, he carried on knocking-up compo.

But he was a fly one, was Tibby — no use sending him to the stores for skyhooks! — and Stoker was not amused when, shortly before knocking-off time, he discovered his bike was missing.

"Whaur's m'bike . . . m'bliddy bike . . . m'bliddy bike . . . .?" he bellowed threateningly, instinctively making a beeline for the carpenter boy.

"How should I know?" growled Tibby. Then, pointing to the house where the duck was lately imprisoned (it had been raffled through the lunch hour break), the site carpenter volunteered, "It was in there the last time I saw it."

Which was true enough, though even given this information, it was ages before the navvy spotted the bike, and no wonder!

Aided and encouraged by Tibby, the lately navvy-fearing apprentices had, with the aid of a jinny wheel, successfully hoisted the bicycle up to the very apex of the high pitched roof, lashing it to a collar and fastening the rope ends to purlin and rafter.

Stoker just couldn't believe it. His mouth dropped open and his eyes widened as, trying to take in the situation, he stared upwards into the dim recesses of the roof space; and the whole gang hurried to the scene to watch him climb the heights and disentangle the machine, which he did, keeping up a running commentary on the origin of all greenhorn tradesmen.

Still smarting under the ankle injury, Tibby ridiculed loudly, derisively, "Whaur's m'bike, m'bliddy bike, m'bliddy bike?"

"Ah dinny ken, ah dinny ken," responded one liberated brickie 'prentice, throwing discretion to the winds, while the other, oddly vernacular, chanted continuously "Och aye, och aye! Och aye the noo!"

Then, "Quack, quack!" called the apprentices in unison, reassured by the presence of the men, and encouraged by their laughter.

"Quack, quack, quack, quack."

When he heard about the incident, the boss was all for sending Tibby straight back to the yard but, as it happened, the inclement weather beat him to it.

It had been a particularly wet season and Lappitt, caught virtually without a roof on, was forced to gather in his men from the sites and, somehow, find employment for them in the yard; priming frames, knocking-up spot boards, repairing the concrete floor to the stores, sieving — through Mrs Lappitt's cast-off silk stockings — the skinned and congealed paint in myriads of tins and kettles, and many other odd jobs not normally given such particular attention. In other words they were expected to make themselves generally useful.

A few even enjoyed the change involved in tackling unfamiliar work, but one and all looked forward especially to the lunch hour natter in the aromatic comfort of the carpenter's shop, undisturbed by the possibility of harrassment from Lappitt who, at that time of day, habitually occupied a barside stool at the *Nags Head*; he was very fond of the landlady's dinerette specials. Mrs Lappitt generally cooked in the evenings and, as she was a keen member of the Womens Institute and other gregarious organisations, it suited her very well to have the whole day to herself, uninterrupted by the nuisance of having to concoct a mid-day meal, she being a weight-watcher who felt exposed to temptation if she sat down to the table on her own.

It was Stoker's turn to fetch the gang's cigarette supplies from the corner shop and, while he was away the apprentices, eager to exploit their newfound retaliatory anti-Stoker powers — and satisfied that Archie, too, was otherwise employed — got busy arranging a little surprise. As a consequence, in the middle of the lunch hour chitchat, unmistakeable duck noises, varying in density from a few odd quacks to the pandemonium of a desperate wingtip-to-tip scuffle, came from the vicinity of the vast heaps of shavings at either end of the carpenter's shop.

The tradesmen were in the habit of egging-on, even baiting, Stoker to get him talking, for once started he was not only voluble but wittily informative, having a vast store of lurid anecdotal reminiscences at his command; and it was while he was holding forth on one of his intricate poaching stories that the first sounds of feathered battle filtered through.

Talk suspended, the men looked askance at one another as the volume of flapping wings and angry squawks rose to a pitch.

The apprentices sat back among the shavings and split their sides, relishing the astonished comical-like expression which took shape on Stoker's ruddy features as he rose to investigate. No sooner did he arrive at one end of the shop, than the kerfuffle stopped, only to restart at the other end. Again and again it happened.

While it lasted, the atmosphere was electric but, of course, with not a duck in sight it was only a matter of time before the mystery was uncovered; whereupon Stoker, realising how thick he had been, ranted and raved at Tibby and his mates, for he, who prided himself on always "seeing the funny side", was not at all keen on having his own leg pulled by junior artisans, or anyone else for that matter.

"I'll show ya, y'buggers," he promised, his face even redder than usual. "Jist you wait till I git y'bawk on that bliddy site! An' wai'll y'r time's up! — we'll see then if y' can tak' y'r med'cine."

Had someone funded a prize for the best ideas on the subject of initiation rites, Stoker would, without question, have walked away with it for, when put into practice, his fertile imaginings on apprentice torture had to be seen to be believed.

His outburst had a sobering effect on the apprentices; the memory of previous initiations lingered on.

Take the case of Jim, a promising lad and handy with the trowel, but much influenced by way-out torsorial trends. Currently, he sported peroxided, shoulder length locks, highlighted with emerald streaks — this at a time when even a Tony Curtis was reckoned outrageous — such affront to nature alternately mesmerising and infuriating Stoker's instinctive conformity to short back and sides.

When Jim's time came, he was cornered by several of the gang who stripped off his clothes, bound him hand and foot, hauled him up a ladder and, using 4″ galvanised clouts, nailed him to the scaffold through the soles of his laced-up fell boots. Arms spread wide, wrists lashed to timber framing, he stood erect in cruciform fashion, birthday-suited, complaining vociferously while astonished passers-by gaped and gasped as Stoker, with obvious relish, turned the hose on him from a vantage point nearby.

Some might say, of course, that such treatment was nothing compared with what happened to Barney, for whom Stoker devised a special, tailor-made rite, taking advantage of special circumstances; at that time the firm was engaged in building a small block of flats on one side of the high street, while rebuilding a shop property opposite.

On this occasion the unfortunate apprentice was again denuded and roped to the scaffold, from where he watched anxiously as his togs were gathered together and removed to the other side of the street. There, for all to see, the bundle was tied to a scaffold pole on the top lift.

A great deal of crude banter ensued as Barney was set free, but after initial hesitation and followed by catcalls and whistles from the gang, he hurriedly scrambled off the scaffold and streaked across the crowded thoroughfare in full view of pedestrians and motorists alike — even shop assistants, alerted by the unusual kerfuffle, coming out to investigate.

It was a scene to be treasured in the memory of all who witnessed it.

Seldom a year went by without at least one or two apprentices going through the hoop for, to his credit, Lappitt determined to do his bit for the trade despite the fact that the best of the lads, after completing their indentures, promptly moved on to pastures new; some, confident of their prowess and eager to break into the big time, joining forces to sub-contract their labour.

While the up-and-coming generation hated his guts, Stoker nevertheless enjoyed a special notoriety in the annals of local initiation, and in the fullness of time even apprentices would profess to see the funny side.

Other firms would stick to oft-repeated traditional rites — like immersion in river or lock, or forced drinking of yards of adulterated pale ale or best bitter — but Lappitt, though affecting a pretence of shock at Stoker's behaviour, nursed a secret pride when, in the *Nag's Head*, his peers questioned him about the latest baptism.

After early drizzle, it turned into a fine evening and Lappitt was reluctant to take his leave of the orchard. Besides, being a worrier, his inside was all of a flather, and he knew from experience that contact with Jack was good for him.

"You were asking what you would do about Tibby? There are times, Sam, when it's best to do nothing, just let nature take its course and sort things out. Stoker'll have to learn to take his medicine if he wants to tangle with Tibby, and as for that tech teacher. . . ." Here, he sounded almost wistful, ". . .I'd've liked to be able to say I'd turned out a Silver Trowel winner, but I know, and that young 'un knows, it's not possible. Just wait till he takes his 'practical'! That'll be the real test."

Surprisingly, the site carpenter had commended Tibby for his carcassing work. "He'll never make a joiner, of course, but he's first rate at roofing and trimming joists, and it's a long time since I saw his like at floor bashin'; he revels in it!"

Although he had eaten far too many cherries, Lappitt,

encouraged by Jack's advice to take no further action, felt much better and smilingly turned to him, "They tell me Tibby's father manages that new radio shop in the high street: hence the tape recorders, I suppose?" His laugh was almost matey, for now the tension had eased, he too could see the funny side.

"Pickstock's answer to Ludwig Koch is Tibby — goes all over the place recording. . . ."

Jack spotted Mary threading her way towards them through the trees, a tea towel on her arm and a coloured beaker in her hand.

"Drop of soup for you, Jack."

She hesitated, then politely asked, "Would you care for some, Mr Lappitt?"

"Oh, no, no, no, I was just off. Thanks all the same."

He got up and looked down at Jack as if there was something still to be said.

The carpenter grinned, "I was coming back on Monday, anyway."

As Lappitt moved off, Jack, spooning his soup, ruminated: Mediterranean cruise! African safari! The man must be going soft in the head.

And what was that bit about old age? Certainly, he was not too old to appreciate the soft swell of Mary's bosom as she stretched to get at a few ripe cherries just out of reach. Speculatively, he watched her. She might be forty, but she wasn't fat. Mature, of course. A fine woman.

Millie had always kept her at arm's length, especially since that time when she'd allowed her to do the washing-up. In Millie's book the most damaging thing one woman could say about another was to condemn her habit of piling all the dirty dishes into the washing-up water in the sink, *knives* and all! The handles were just bound to fall off.

"What'll it be then, Mary," Jack asked, taking out his

penny whistle. "Colonel Bogey?"

He had been watching the style of her as, both arms raised, she tinkered with the bun at the nape of her neck, and before she could respond to his question, he quickly put aside the whistle and, patting his breast pocket, informed her, "I've still got some cherry money left. Come on and we'll have a jar at the *Diggers.*"

The Managing Kind

NO man is more insufferable than the newly converted, be his discovery merely commonplace like, for example, the merits of a high fibre bran intake, cleaning teeth with a particular brand of toothpaste, giving up smoking or, for that matter, changing political direction when confronted by the thoughts of Chairman Mao or some other stone-age Keir Hardy.

Anyone of this persuasion takes an inordinate revulsion to those of us still unconverted to those sometimes desirable practices, berating us unmercifully as though such items of diet, personal hygiene or political precepts were second nature to him; habits of a lifetime.

Some such thoughts had been rummaging around in Duggie's mind since his father took him to task for failing to attend church on Sunday. This despite the fact that his own churchgoing dated only from last Easter's commemoration, a longing for his native heath awakening the Presbyterian soul in him.

Hitherto a steadfast free thinker, the father was a man who expected from all members of this Anglo-Irish family, reasonable compliance with his wishes and, although the teenage offspring had the same permissive instincts as others of his generation, paternal control was balanced and effective.

So, the day word came from Londonderry that Duggie's grandmother had departed this life, the father, anxious to promote the church connection, extracted a promise that, in the absence of the rest of the family at the funeral, he would at least attend the young peoples' fellowship outing arranged for the weekend.

Wishing he had something better to do, Duggie nevertheless arrived at the appointed meeting place resolved to take his medicine with as good a grace as possible.

And that was when it all really began, one thing triggering another; the domino effect.

He had been waiting only a couple of minutes when, swivelling abruptly on his heel, he collided awkwardly with a girl who had just stepped across the grass verge, causing her to stumble and almost fall to the ground.

Quickly recovering, he steadied her with an outstretched arm, at the same time noticing that, although a slim slip of a girl, she was exceedingly good looking and well contoured, with a mop of attractive, light brown hair. Apologising profusely for his clumsiness, he again looked her over, and the more he looked, the more he was possessed by a tingling, excited admiration.

Dropping her eyes to his continued stare, she reassured him.

"I'm all right, really I am." Then, glancing shyly, "you'll be one of Mr Terry's party?"

He was.

"They call me Ginny," she said, extending a hand.

He was quite overcome and, when in due course the Rev. Terry gathered together the rest of the party and marched them all down the lane to the nature reserve, Duggie proceeded to follow Ginny about for the rest of the afternoon, even contriving to be alone with her in the middle of a nursery conifer plantation, where he stammered out his conviction that she was the prettiest thing ever to come out of Pickstock. A clear case of assault and flattery!

When, later, he thought about it, Duggie had no clear recollection as to just how it came about that Ginny had walked him home in the mid-evening, accepted with alacrity a rather tentative invitation to supper, then helped him consume most of the home-made potted meat his mother had left to see him through the week-end.

Their impact on one another had been instantaneous and both sensed this was to be much more than mere casual acquaintanceship.

She seemed a shy, doelike creature, but in fact was a born manager, in her quiet way ready for a challenge from whatever quarter it came. Clever, too! Lately enrolled at a teacher training college, she had collected three 'A' levels on the way and had her sights clearly focussed on an academic career.

After they had finished eating, they cleared away and lost no time in flopping into each other's arms on the front room sofa, a hard, Victorian straight-laced article that soon drove them to seek solace upstairs in the best bedroom. The evening being chilly, they were not loathe to slip between the sheets.

Courting novices they might be, but they brushed immaturity aside in an intensity of feeling quite new to both of them. The Rev. Terry's outing was to serve more than its intended purpose; for them, a red letter day long to be remembered.

Before meeting Duggie, Ginny had called at a shop in the high street to pick up a tape she had ordered. It was *Baroque Organ Works*, which included her favourite Albinoni's *Adagio*, and now, as they settled down, they listened to the music on Duggie's portable recorder — which had a sobering effect, for the moment cooling desire as if to remind them that they were rushing through their romantic overtures much too quickly. They were finely tuned to one another from the start, already at ease and, involuntarily, Duggie leaned over, pecked her on the nose, and giving himself up to the music which was new to him, reflected quietly as he took her hand in his, "Wouldn't my old man be mad if he could see us now!" He smiled. "Mind you, we've him to thank for this. We'd probably never even have met if he hadn't pushed me into going on the outing. What a laugh!"

"Strikes me your father knows what's good for you."

"Of course. He wants to steer me away from my mates on the sites: bad influence and all that. . . . He's not forgiven me for preferring a bricklaying apprenticeship to working in the bank."

He turned to her, smoothed her brow and kissed her chastely.

"You don't mind me being a manual worker, do you, Ginny? I'm reasonably educated and all that. I'm in the last year of my indentures and I intend to get on. But . . . you know how folk talk about class — working-class, middle-class and all that cod — well, lately, I've discovered the class I belong to, and that's the kitchen class."

"Duggie! Whatever do you mean?"

"Well, when I'm in the house on my own, I often go into the kitchen and pour myself a can of beer or a coke, and it's in the kitchen I listen to the radio or my tape recorder, or do my swotting for Monday's tech. And each time I hop on to the worktop, I say to myself, 'Duggie,' I say, 'you're a kitchen man pure and simple'."

Her hair cascaded over the pillow as she tugged it free from its ornamental clip. Putting an arm round his neck, she pulled him down towards her.

"I do love you, Duggie. You might not have any 'A' levels, but you're streets ahead of me, much more mature. I think we were made for each other."

The tape clicked off as he took her in his arms.

He had often heard his mates rabbiting on about sex — even more than booze and football. It was their consuming passion. In the site shed, pictures of girls topless and top heavy festooned the walls. Of course, he had his appetites like the rest of them but, all the same, had wondered what all the fuss was about, especially when he came to realise that those who had most to contribute on the subject were often the least experienced — like the plumber apprentice, a pimply, gangling youth full of lurid tales of sex in the raw, who would have given anything just to take a girl to the pictures.

And here he was, Duggie, about to experience the ultimate!

It was a long time before they surfaced; when they did, Ginny was the first to take in the situation. Something would have to be done.

"We'll have to get the washing machine out. You *have* got a washing machine? I think perhaps it would be as well if we steeped the sheets in cold water first. I've seen my mum do that. Then we'll wash 'as directed'. When they're dry, I'll give them a good iron and *nobody'll* be any the wiser."

Life was full of contrast, mused Duggie. Together they had journeyed into the unknown, had explored this wonderful ecstatic world of love and passion; now, here was Ginny showing the other side of the coin — sheer practicality.

He wondered how on earth she could stay so calm. She was a marvellous girl but no longer Virginia intacta; he had come across the phrase somewhere and now refashioned it to suit. Remarkably, Ginny continued to be not in the least concerned. For sheer grit and nerve, she took the biscuit!

Gazing dreamily at the ceiling and pursing her lips in mock contrition, she whispered coyly, "I'll see it doesn't happen again, Duggie darling."

He couldn't help but smile, though, as he gave her an affectionate hug he came very near to panic. What a fathead he'd been to use the best bedroom!

"But what are we going to do," he queried, a trace of anxiety creeping into his voice as he threw back the sheets.

He felt nothing like as mature as she sounded and, although secretively rather pleased with himself, kept on thinking about what his father would say (or do?) if only he could see his Duggie now.

"The main thing is not to panic," he heard her say. "Everything is possible if you don't panic — that's what my mum always says. Now, Duggie, you nip into the bathroom and half fill the bath."

Just as she had predicted, the process was entirely successful, and the twin tub in the scullery finished the job nicely.

"They'll dry in no time in this stiff breeze," Ginny remarked afterwards as she finished pegging out the washing on the line.

A gibbous moon slid from behind a cloud and lit up the garden as the sheets, cracking away like rifle shots, alerted the woman next door who, draping an old mackintosh around her shoulders, came shambling to the fence, amazed and puzzled by the late night spectacle. Right enough, she had promised Duggie's mother to keep an eye on him, but this seemed something quite beyond her remit, something she hadn't bargained for.

As luck would have it, by this time the pair had already regained the privacy of the kitchen, and the woman, shaking her head and shrugging, clip-clopped over the flags and back indoors, determined that in the morning she would enlist Duggie's help with her enquiries.

"Leave them out until they're quite dry," advised Ginny, "and don't forget to bring them in later on and fold as best you can. I'll see to the ironing and make up the bed again before your folks come back."

"That'll give Nosey Annie next door something to clack about," exulted Duggie.

He lifted Ginny off her feet and planted a final kiss before setting her down. Then he chased her through the hallway to the front door and walked her home to the other side of town, saying his goodbyes discreetly at the gate.

When a sudden elation welled up within him, he raced back pell mell through the sombre streets, leaving the odd late-night moocher staring after him wonderingly.

Home again, he sat on the bottom tread of the stairs. The kitchen door was open. He'd put on the Albinoni which Ginny had left behind, and he was thinking that this was his exact position in the scheme of things . . . a long way from the lounge.

Their next open air meeting again proved to be something of an introductory experience for Ginny. She had a close chum, Doris, who was acquainted with a workmate of Duggie's, one Henry Sanders, labourer and stand-in lorry driver for Lappitt. An evening foursome was arranged, the girls to be picked up on Boots' corner at eight sharp.

The rush hour traffic long since abated, at the appointed hour the two girls waiting on the street corner watched the approach of a solitary vehicle snorting its way past Woolies, obviously hard pressed to master the sharp incline to the crossroads. Not that the girls had ever before evinced curiosity in transporters or, for that matter, industrial or commercial stock of any kind, hydraulic or otherwise, but there was nothing else in sight to hold their attention.

Surely, they speculated idly, the lone trundler must be heading for a last resting place in Johnson's auto necropolis straight ahead down the Hanley road. But no, as it drew abreast it actually shuddered to a halt, gave a final consumptive cough and from its nether regions relieved itself of a cloud of black, poisonous vapour.

Henry, who had been banking on borrowing for the occasion his mechanic brother's souped-up jalopy, had found him bent on a date of his own and, consequently, the jalopy was not available. Duggie was in a great state when he heard this, for he had been looking forward to sitting on the back seat close to his newfound love.

"Leave it to me," Henry had consoled. "I'll fix it somehow." Hence the last minute clandestine conscription of Lappitt's geriatric vehicle for duty as a potential chariot d'amour.

Pressurised by Parsley Jack's perpetual grousing that the lorry was cluttering up the yard, Lappitt had for some time past been half-heartedly trying to sell it. The trouble was that he felt somewhat attached to the thing, which was already a veteran when acquired just after the war. He regarded it almost as a mascot, the same as other people do who possess lucky medallions or pennies or rabbits' feet, so he had clung to possession, evaluating the lorry as a talisman that had seen him through many difficult times over the years.

In the first place it had been bought to cart bricks when circumstances in the fletton yards forced him to find his own means of transportation and, having served him well for many years, he looked on it as a good and faithful servant. Even after being forced to buy a brand new replacement he felt churlish and awkward at having to get rid of it. There ought, he reasoned, to be some way of pensioning off such a loyal retainer, some way of putting it out to grass like you'd do a worn out nag.

Often the lorry driver remarked on Sam's concern for inanimate objects, giving it as his opinion that they were better thought of than the establishment flesh and blood.

Yet, even in decline — unlovely and unwashed — it still did service as the yard rubbish skip, with an occasional run round the sites when No. 1 was at the garage for maintenance or repair.

"You might have some chance of selling it if you had it spruced up a bit," Parsley had suggested, but to no avail.

The girls, wide-eyed, stared unbelievingly as the athletic figure of Henry leapt smartly from the cab. Then, once again, they turned their attention to the battered old wreck. It was some time before they recovered their wits sufficiently to grasp what was expected of them. Doris especially, was flabbergasted and looked as though she couldn't make up her mind whether to laugh or cry. She was the first to speak.

"You don't mean . . . you can't think . . . do you really expect. . . ?"

Words failed. Ginny continued speechless, looking aghast at the flaking paintwork and mud-caked wheels.

Duggie had joined Henry on the pavement, eyes only for Ginny.

"Well," coaxed Henry, casting a protective glance at Lappitt's pride and joy, "you'll find it ain't as bad as it looks, really you will. The cab holds four comfortable, honest it does!"

Unconcerned as to the cab's seating capacity, Doris countered sourly, "Henry Sanders! If you think we're gonna get into that filthy old tub, you've got another think comin'. Why! what d'ye think my mum 'ud say? What a cheek! expectin' us to . . . well, I never!"

One or two passersby looked askance, taking in the situation and coming to their own conclusions. There was something frightening, sexually malevolent about a lorry driver enticing girls into his cab in broad daylight.

Geriatric lorry-cum-chariot d'amour

Stories about females buttonholed and carried off for unmentionable nefarious purposes stirred and rankled in the subconscious.

Doris took Ginny by the arm and in high dudgeon, was about to fire her parting shot when Henry, lowering his voice to a hoarse agitated whisper, pleaded.

"Doris! there's a cop comin'. For god's sake get in quick and let's go."

She turned, saw a policeman rounding Woolworth's corner and, after hesitating momentarily, with a toss of the head reluctantly complied, scrambling aboard and signalling Ginny to follow, Duggie bundling in behind.

In the back of the lorry alongside a clapped-out, redundant concrete mixer inadequately secured, defective scaffold boards, fittings and an assortment of builders' rubbish cluttered and bumped around the metal-lined floor, adding to the general hubub as the elderly crock chugged and wheezed down the main street, heading for open country.

Glumly, the girls stared ahead through the windscreen, finding it almost impossible to keep their balance, for the cab seat bucked, lurched and slid about like a cakewalk at a fair. Raising his voice above the general clatter, Henry, with mock solemnity, reasoned, "I don't know why folks get so stuck on Jags and Mercedes. What could be better than this? Eh? What say, Duggie?" Deadly serious, he cocked his head and waited for a reply.

Trying hard to preserve her po-faced expression, Doris gave him a shove that almost landed the lorry in a ditch. But the ice was broken, and laughing and shouting to one another, they began to think it a great lark. Ginny, despite Duggie's attentions, slid off the seat altogether, landing in a heap on the cab floor, but by this time they were all on the giggle and Henry, to keep control, was forced to change noisily down to a lower gear till the fit subsided.

Had he not been bent on an errand of charity, Lappitt would not that evening have taken his refreshment at the *Brickmaker's Arms*.

The men on the jobs had had a whip round for Alec who, although an indifferent bricklayer, was a diligent worker, a likeable, generous man popular with everyone. He had suffered a blockage in his back passage and, after a bad post-operational spell, was making a good recovery.

Lappitt had added his own quite generous contribution to the collection — in recent times he had been seen to be rather more free with his money — and had been deputed to call at Alec's home and hand it over.

The patient was obviously much improved, so much so that, being anxious to renew acquaintance with the local brew, he found little difficulty in persuading Lappitt to accompany him to the *Brickmaker's*, only a stone's throw down the lane. Money being tight, Alec's wife had not been too sure about licencing this return to normality. So, for a time, she effectively delayed their departure by insisting on Sam taking a cup of tea and sampling her newly-baked treacle scones; this he was quite pleased to do because he had not eaten since lunchtime and had arranged a late dinner, his wife having gone off for the day on a townswomens' guild outing.

As he wiped the crumbs from his whiskers, he looked around the cosy little kitchen, noting the budgie chunnering away in its gilded cage, and Margery, the teenage mongol only child, sitting by the kitchen stove fiddling with a box of dominoes and a packet of playing cards, the real purpose of which she would never know.

Sam's social conscience took off on one of its rare flights, so much so that looking from child to mother he enquired gently, "Are you able to get out much? And what about schooling?"

Ivy was a wiry grey haired woman who, for fifty years, had borne with fortitude the cross of an exceedingly hirsute visage; though, as if in compensation, God had given her a magnificent torso which, in her early days on fancy dress occasions, she exploited to the full by entering as an Arab slave girl, yashmak firmly secured with tape and glue, to be voted — except by the less well endowed — the belle of the ball.

She answered Sam mildly.

"Oh, yes, we manage well enough, you know. We've got very good neighbours and Margery goes to the convent school for a few hours three mornings a week, don't you Marge?"

At first the child responded vacantly, then produced a gutteral untranslatable explosion. A broad grin creased her features only to vanish instantly as she turned once more to her play.

This performance unsettled Sam. Why, he wondered, did people have to get married at all? There was no need for it. He could remember that when he got married he thought of all the privileges he had to forgo — like spending his own money, lying by the wall in the double bed and sitting next to the window in bus or train.

Ivy rose, gave him another cup of tea and handed Margery a chocolate biscuit.

"My Marge is a loving child, Mr Lappitt. No one will ever know how often I've thanked the Lord for giving me the blessing of her company. Can I help you to another scone? I'm quite famous for my scones, at least, so Alec tells me. Does your wife keep well, Mr Lappitt? I heard some weeks ago that she had to attend the clinic for her arthritis. A great handicap is that complaint."

Such a thoughtful, cordial woman! Still, Sam reflected, when you've got a physog like hers you'd have to work twice as hard at the social graces — everybody else having a head start.

Instantly recognising the iniquity of the thought, and partly in penance, he took out his wallet and handed Ivy a five-pound note.

"I'd like you to buy something for yourself and Margery — a treat. Will you do that to pleasure me?"

Ivy protested that having been given one hand-out there was no call for another. But Sam was adamant, determined to offset the slip of his thinking.

Whereupon, Alec rose gingerly from his chair. "Come on, then, if we're going. You can leave your car here, Sam, it'll save me the bother of getting in and out."

Ivy and Margery were still very much on Sam's mind when the two men entered the pub, and after they sat down with their drinks, he returned to his questioning. "Tell me, Alec, how does Ivy cope with a child like that?"

"Well, maybe she's no oil painting, my Ivy, but she's a wonderful wife and mother. It's not easy managing someone like Margery, but Ivy's the managing kind — keeps the house spotless, as you'd see, and is a marvellous cook. I'm no oil painting myself, so I suppose we're two of a kind. We're happy enough."

"It must have been difficult for you these last few weeks with little or nothing coming in?"

"Ivy works at Timson's cafe three mornings a week. That brings in a few pounds and, give her her due, Mrs Timson is very appreciative."

"I suppose you could've put the child in a home?"

"What! Ivy wouldn't hear of it. Neither would I . . . now."

After a couple of drinks Sam went out to the gents, on the way passing the lounge door through which he was surprised to see Duggie and Henry sitting with the two girls.

"Hullo! hullo! Wot you two up to, then?"

He noticed immediately that the atmosphere was distinctly tense, which puzzled him a bit. Certainly, Henry was not the flamboyant Henry Sam knew him to be. They seemed to be quite taken aback by his sudden appearance and, had he not known better, he would have put it down to self-consciousness, a backwardness at being discovered by the boss in female company in an out of the way pub. Henry piped up, obviously making an effort at offhand communication, "Just having a quiet drink with our girlfriends, Mr Lappitt."

Sam noted that the two girls were real bobby dazzlers and, expansively, took a note from his pocket and put it down on the table.

"Ave a drink on me — an' don't do anything I wouldn't do!" he admonished, cocking his head and smirking.

It was a few minutes before he returned to the saloon bar.

"You got a job round here, Sam?" Alec enquired.

"No. Why?"

"Could've sworn that was our old lorry I see backing out of the pub yard a couple of minutes ago."

"Never! You must have bin mistaken."

Thoughtfully, Sam emptied his glass and went up to the bar, on the way glancing out of the window. Then, as the barman refilled the glasses, on the spur of the moment, he went out and popped his head round the corner of the lounge door.

Gone! Vamoosed! Scarpered! So that was it! But in the lorry? No wonder they'd been nervous. If only he'd had his car outside he could have raced them back to base, but it was too late now.

There were times when he was very good at putting

two and two together. He was jumping to conclusions, of course, but he knew well enough when to trust his intuition.

Fuming, he sat down again, his research into the bricklayer's domestic affairs entirely forgotten.

Abruptly, he drank up, walked Alec home and, impatient to get back into town, asked him to say goodbye to Ivy for him.

The following day, the boyos, summoned to HQ, were shown into the back room to find Lappitt in a filthy temper since, on his morning rounds, he had stopped off at the council site to be greeted by Dick, the working foreman.

"Factory inspector's bin 'ere."

"Oh?"

"Says he's gonna pinch us for contravening the scaffolding regs."

"Bloody hell! Wot yer done?"

"No guardrail or toeboards round that chimney," explained Dick half sheepishly, pointing with his thumb.

"Bloody hell!"

The foreman, seeking to appease his boss by adopting a wheedling whine, countered, "Well, 'e come sneakin' on us unawares. We was just finishing off, almost ready to strip down. Another few minutes. . . ."

"Hard luck! Is that what you want me to think?"

Pacing up and down, Lappitt was uncertain as to his next move.

"Made a right ol' cock-up, ain't ya?"

The normal run of site problems and checks on material supplies were forgotten. Frustrated by Dick's unwillingness to parley further, he again exploded, "Bloody hell!"

Disgusted, he turned on his heel and marched back to

the truck, but goaded and emboldened by the patent negligence of the foreman, shouted at him over his shoulder, "You stupid bugger! You'll be the ruination of me yet."

He revved the engine furiously and nursed his tantrum all the way back to the yard. There could be a court case, of course, with all its attendant anxieties.

Now, scowling, he examined the delinquents standing by his desk with their hands behind their backs. Though not exactly at ease, their demeanour showed only a modicum of concern.

Still wearing his porkpie hat, he cleaned his half-moon reading spectacles with paper from a toilet roll kept in the bottom drawer, sited them carefully on the inadequate bridge of his snub nose, placed both hands on the edge of the desk and, confidently assuming the manner of a Crown Court prosecutor, peered at the lads owlishly, yet still without saying a word. He had found this procedure very effective when formally carpeting any of his employees; there was something especially intimidating about the specs which in fact were twenty years old and totally useless for any other purpose.

"I hope you're not going to waste my time by denying you were pub crawlin' with our ol' lorry last night? It would be useless, I assure you. The engine was still red hot when I got back from the *Brickmaker's*." He paused. "Can either of you give me one good reason why I shouldn't sack the pair of you here and now?"

This produced an uneasy silence.

"Well, what d'ye say? Speak up! You, Henry, you've always got plenty to say for yourself; not exactly the tongue-tied type."

He searched their faces for some glimmer of reaction.

". . . An' what about insurance? What d'ye think the insurance company 'ud 'ave to say? Suppose you'd had an accident? Didn't think of that, I'll be bound?"

This, too, produced no response. Irrelevantly, he continued. "Don't think I don't know what goes on. I haven't been in the building trade all these years without learning some of the tricks you get up to!"

He stuck his chin out aggressively, a sign that he was quite sure of himself and intent on pressing home his advantage.

Henry, however, knew only too well when to keep his mouth shut, thus forcing Lappitt to vent his spleen until, for lack of friction, he ran out of steam altogether. Henry had advised Duggie to closely follow his example and say as little as possible. Nevertheless, he decided it was time to play the contrite bit.

"Sorry, Mr Lappitt. It won't happen again."

"You're dead right it won't happen again! Why! it's all over town: Lappitt's passion wagon, they're calling it — amongst other things. Bloody cheek! How would you feel if you was in my shoes? I'll never be able to show my face in the *Brickmaker's* again."

Henry, though he wanted to laugh out loud — "don't do anything I wouldn't do" kept ringing in his ears — controlled himself sufficiently to perform an awkward shuffle. Duggie, meanwhile, was tortured by recollection in sound and vision of the return journey of the decrepit old crock down Pickstock high street — loose scaffolding and cement mixer raising all hell in the back — with the girls, laughing hysterically, alternately leaning precariously out of the cab windows and appealing to Henry to stop and let them get off.

"I expect you'd have taken the new one if it hadn't been under lock and key," Lappitt growled. "You realise there's not another builder in Pickstock who wouldn't sack you on the spot?"

This, too, elicited no response, though they were both well aware of the truth of the statement.

Lappitt, glowering ferociously, threateningly,

wondering what tack to take next, was struck by a sudden thought.

"You, Duggie! What d'ye think your father 'ud say? and you not out of your indentures yet?"

Sobered by the thought, Duggie eyed the carpet.

"And Henry, in future you'll hand all the keys in at the office when you knock off."

Of course he had no intention of sacking them. They were two of the best young prospects he had engaged for years; good workers, good enough to be snapped up by Thomson or Wheeler if shown the door. But he had to assert his authority. There would be no living with it if he didn't get the message across that he would not stand for anyone playing fast and loose with the firm's property. The cheek! Imagine parking the thing outside one of his favourite pubs!

He recalled other occasions when he'd had to warn men, good men at that, to keep their hands off his plant after hours, men doing outside jobs without as much as a by-your-leave. Moonlighting, he'd heard it called. Once, he'd had to get rid of an entire gang when he found painters working the long summer evenings and weekends doing jobs on their own account, using his ladders and trestles, even his brushes — the best that money could buy — perhaps his paint as well, though he couldn't prove it. But some of the surrogate sub-contractors he engaged were little better, and often he wondered if he'd just swopped one problem for another.

The recollection of it all got his blood pressure going, and his knuckles showed white against the mahogany edging of the desk as he gripped hard to rein a rising malignancy.

"I'll be on you like a load o' bricks. . . ." he began finally, only to be interrupted by sounds of a rumpus in the outer office, and in burst Dick, breathing heavily.

"I wants me cards," he announced loudly, oblivious of what was afoot and fixing Lappitt with a hostile, challenging glare.

"Bloody hell," exclaimed Lappitt, removing his specs and slumping back in his chair.

The Perfectionist

THE teenage girl with the grey tinted hair stared fixedly at her mother chatting-up elderly blue-rinsed acquaintances who were trying hard to get a word in. She stood a little apart from the group on the high street pavement, the generation gap exemplified in her diffident, special kind of detachment — the thin, fine critical look of the newly aware female.

Relishing his lunchtime bait, Ted sat dangling his feet over the scaffolding two storeys up, surveying the scene with speculative interest, wondering who was who and what all the rabbiting was about. He divided his attention between the gossiping women and a young couple standing immediately below whom he would have liked to move over a bit so that they could at least present something of an elevational perspective instead of the less informative head and shoulders plan.

But his attention was entirely diverted when he heard a high-pitched querulous voice exhorting the world at large to count its blessings, in the wake of which, round the corner from Waterloo Street, came a ragged old woman in a Marie Lloyd hat, arms flaying in a semaphore fashion which she evidently imagined to be appropriately theatrical. He could see she was intent on supplementing her old age pension; a leftover urge from the in-between-the-war years, pursuing a way of life she had found hard to give up.

Suddenly, a few feet from where Ted sat, a box sash was noisily thrown up and a brash young insurance clerk poked his head out of the window and shouted at the Marie Lloyd figure, "Aw, belt up, you noisy old bag!" saying which, he flung a few coppers down at her. One must have found its mark because the hymn singing stopped abruptly.

Just as the window slammed shut again, Ted pulled himself erect on to the scaffold. The timing was unfortunate because the old woman, not entirely appreciative of the insurance alms, immediately associated Ted with the assault and, incensed, aimed a stream of gutter invective in his direction. Taken aback, the innocent carpenter gaped in bewilderment at being thus hauled willy nilly into the act.

A few minutes later, Lappitt, turning the corner, spotted Ted, now at the foot of the scaffold and in hot dispute with Marie Lloyd. Without a moment's hesitation he quickened his pace, crossed the road and, pressing a coin into the old girl's hand, told her in no uncertain manner to "'Op it, 'fore I call the cops". He was well acquainted with Marie, a local character whom he considered a blot on the community, and he needed no briefing as to the circumstances leading to the incident, aware that trouble followed wherever she went. Quite satisfied with her interlude, the old girl shambled off, breaking into the one and only hymn in her repertoire, counting her blessings with renewed vigour.

"How gettin' on, Ted?"

"All right, Mr Lappitt, except for the old girl." He grinned. "One thing, though, can you tell me if I'm to renew those sash cords front *and* back? — they're all dickey. And what about that rotten window frame in the bathroom? and the bedroom doors? — nearly all loose on their hinges — panels cracked — want replacing."

"Ah, well, we'll have to see 'bout that. You can do the sashes all round, but I'll have to find out 'bout the winder and doors. I'm seeing Mr Bowles later on; promised his wife to look in on him at the hospital to cheer him up a bit."

Ted couldn't help wondering how the cheering-up was to be accomplished because, having met Bowles before his accident, he knew that he and Lappitt were two of a kind and hardly likely to set the ward alight.

"Let's have a look at what you've bin doin', then."

No doubt about it, thought Sam as he examined the work, this chap was the daddy of them all, best tradesman he'd ever had in his employ. He could scribe a board to a deviating member so that it was quite impossible to detect, or put a warped door in purgatory to reproduce perfection. And he was quite different from the other chaps, so well spoken and polite. But the *time* he was taking! Bowlsey would do his nut when he got the bill, despite what he had said.

Reluctant as always to take on daywork, he'd been forced into it because the premises were run-down almost to the point of dereliction. The client had inherited the shop with accommodation over when his bachelor brother died suddenly, leaving an ironmongery business which he very soon discovered wasn't worth a light; so he wound it up and determined to titivate and sell the property to the highest bidder.

"Put it into shape for me, Sam," Bowles had said vaguely.

It was over two months since, by a fortuitous circumstance — or so Sam thought at the time — Ted had walked into the office and asked for a job, and as there was a shortage of carpenters and the preliminary shop work was mostly in that line, he had been delighted to take him on.

So here he was, still at it. It had been difficult to know just where to start for the neglect was widespread inside and out, and how founder-Bowles, the deceased's late pernickety father, would have reacted didn't bear thinking about.

Pressed by Bowles to get on with it pronto, the work

had been started even before the rather sketchy list of remedial items had been agreed. Then the farmer had his tractor accident as a result of which he had a foot amputated. Even before that, he had words with Lappitt when he overheard him telling Ted to "get a bloody move on with the job".

"You can't talk to a man like that," Bowles had protested. "That chap's a craftsman, got pride in his work."

Lappitt was staggered at this blatant interference. Never before had a customer taken sides in this way, and Bowles of all people! Always one for his pound of flesh. Angered, he retorted, "All right, all right Cliff! It's your money I'm trying to save, so don't blame me if the bill's not to your liking."

He knew only too well from experience that the bill would be too much whatever it came to. It was always the same with farmers; a mean, cantankerous lot! He'd done work for them before. It was a chancy business and you were lucky to come out of it without losing money.

He would never have taken the work on had it not been for a very special ulterior motive. Mind you, he reflected again, this carpenter certainly was something, no question but that he was used to good quality work — quite an education to watch him perform. It would be marvellous if he could afford to keep him. If only he would sharpen up a bit!

Ted was a fine looking young man, tall, fair and pleasant. A North country product, he told Lappitt he had worked for some time with a firm specialising in purpose-made joinery, after serving an apprenticeship with a Newcastle builder with sites all over Tyneside. Then the recession crept in. He could see the work drying up, so applied for a post teaching carpentry and joinery at the tech school that he attended one day a week when serving his time; but although he was short-listed, he heard nothing more. So, he packed in his job. Idling around and marking time was not to his liking.

His widowed mother begged him to stay in the North, but at twenty four he reckoned his tide was at the flood. It was a big decision to make. Never before had he been further south than Sunderland, and to him any place outside a thirty mile radius of home was the back of beyond. He made up his mind and not even his mother could dissuade him.

As many a one had done before him, he set out for the South humping his little kit of preconceptions, inhibitions, ideas and idealisms, miscellaneous knowledge, carpentry tools and sundries. Sticking a pin into a map of the Home Counties — where else was so much owned by so many? — he presented himself to Pickstock and Lappitt as luck dictated, ready and willing to put all to the test of fortune and acclaim.

He knew very well it would be a risky business digging up roots, but just couldn't wait to see what happened when he cast his bread upon the waters. Anyway, it was much more exciting than waiting for the sack in South Shields.

Of course, he knew that not everybody made a go of things, that many fell by the wayside. But some did get a glimpse of the City Bountiful. His time, he felt, had come, come what may.

Pickstock might not be everybody's idea of the City Bountiful, not Lappitt Ted's choice as Minister of Works. The first sight of Sam's premises, a builder's yard in consummate disarray, almost sent him scurrying back to King's Cross. However, since he had come this far, he decided to stick it out and face the consequences.

At the hospital Lappitt found Bowles even less socially inclined than usual, which was saying something. So there was very little cheering-up done and he passed the time nibbling some salted peanuts he found loose under the torn lining of his jacket pocket.

The farmer wasn't in the mood for talking business and said so.

His wife, Grace, a good looking, slightly built, nice little woman with an attractive cast in one eye, had upset him by getting all emotional about his foot when she came in to see him earlier in the afternoon; this, notwithstanding the fact that for weeks past she had taken it all very well.

Sitting by his bedside, she had suddenly burst into tears.

"It's all right, Grace," he comforted her. "It's getting much better now, and I'll be able to walk okay — you'll see!"

But she was not so easily pacified.

"What is the matter, Grace? What's up?"

"Oh, Cliff, you had such lovely feet!"

"Grace, for god's sake!" He squinted furtively round to see if the man in the next bed had been listening. Then, making an effort, he said brightly, "I've still got one left."

After a while she dried her tears on one of his paper hankies and sat quietly staring at the floor. He could see that something was still troubling her. Eventually, clasping her hands tidily in her lap, she turned to him.

"And what's happened to the foot?"

"What do you mean?"

"You know what I mean. What did they do with it?"

"Oh, I see. Wrapped it in a plastic bag, I suppose, and bunged it in the incinerator."

Her eyes widened. She grabbed hold of the bedclothes. Again she burst into tears. Between sobs, she stammered out, "They'd no right to dispose of it without our permission. After all, we might have wanted to keep it . . . to have it. . . ."

"Embalmed . . . or something? So's we could keep it on the mantelpiece? Oh, Grace . . . really!"

He laughed and tried to put his arm around her, but she was inconsolable.

Of course, he said nothing of this to Lappitt, but the incident had left him out of sorts and he was not in the mood to parley.

"When they lettin' you out, then?" Lappitt enquired finally, picking his teeth.

"Dunno. End of the week, maybe."

"Right! I'll phone Grace on Saturday. See you beginning of next week . . . if you're up to it."

Though nothing had been said at the hospital, Lappitt knew that recently Bowles had received outline planning consent for the residential development of a three acre meadow touching the west end of the town. The application had been bouncing about between him and the planners for over a year. This, more than the shop job, was on Sam's mind when he went to the farm armed with time sheets and invoices, the reaction to which was entirely predictable.

"No use your bringing them bloody things 'ere. I'm in no condition to inspect your books. Just tell me how much it comes to."

Bowles puffed furiously at his pipe as if to signal his no-nonsense disposition.

Of course, Sam had done his sums before calling at the farmhouse. Nevertheless, embarrassed as always when dealing with accounts, he shilly-shallied for a bit, making heavy weather of enumerating and describing the work done, until he realised that the farmer was having a hard time suppressing his impatience. Abandoning explanation he came to the point.

"Within a few pounds — without profit and establishment charges, mind you — it's just under five hundred pounds to date, including materials, of course."

"What! Where d'you think I'm going to lay my hands on that kind of money? Eh? Why, it's more than twice what I'd expected, and not done yet! How much longer you gonna be?"

"Well, given a bit of luck with the weather, Cliff — remember, we've still got the outside to render — and if we get the doors, units and the rest of the stuff early next week as I've bin promised, I should say a month would more or less break the back of it."

"What! Break the back of it! I should hope the bloody job would be finished long before that. I'm advertising it in the property section of the *Courier* week after next."

Grace came in with a pot of tea, poured out two cups and retired to the kitchen. Following on Bowles' stated intention to advertise the shop premises for sale, the two men settled into a discussion on the merits and demerits of the estate agents in the district, grumbling at charges and questioning surveying qualifications. When the subject lapsed, Bowles busied himself re-lighting his pipe.

"Nice lot of pigs you got down in that bottom meader," Sam complimented, going off at a tangent. "I was admiring them as I came past."

Bowles' eyes narrowed, and it was at this juncture that he asked Sam to fetch the whisky bottle and glasses from the sideboard.

"Try the malt," he suggested, suddenly prodigal. "I think you'll find it to your taste."

Encouraged by the mention of his stock, he went on to talk about farming generally and pigs in particular, to Lappitt's surprise actually admitting to having made a nice fat profit on pig farming in recent times. He expected, so he said, to be taking several prizes with his Middle Whites at the agricultural show in July.

"Finest lot I've had in twenty years," he boasted.

"Unfortunately, as you can imagine, I'm going to be a bit handicapped with this leg of mine in the months to come. I'll have to cut down on the workload somewhere along the line."

He puffed at his pipe and told Sam to help himself to another whisky.

"I'm surprised, Sam, you've never tried your hand at a bit of farming? Just the type, I should have thought."

Gratified with the assessment, Sam confessed to having a hankering in that direction, with a predilection for stock farming. He'd just never had the opportunity, he supposed.

Bowles composed his features into something approaching a smile.

"What's to stop you? Why don't you have a go, Sam?"

Then, as Lappitt opened his mouth to reply, the farmer made his bid.

"Tell you what I'll do, Sam! I'll give you four hundred pounds for the complete shop job, and pay the rest of the bill in pigs; that'll get you started. Why not! Are you game? It 'ud make a nice little sideline for you, and very profitable. What d'ye say?"

Lappitt demurred, making garbled noises through his droopy whiskers, producing nothing intelligible because when the pigs were mentioned the whisky went down the wrong way.

"You got plenty of odd bits of ground big enough for a few pigs, I'll be bound. Come to think of it, you got bags of room in that yard of yours, ain't ya?"

Lappitt was non-committal. But he liked playing with the idea of the farming life, turning it over in his mind as another man might make fantasy arrangements in mid-winter for summer holidays in romantic faraway places. Just the same, he would have refused outright, but the trouble was that three acre field. He must come

The rest of the bill was paid in pigs

to grips before Bowlsey got in tow with the agents: level, gravel-bottomed, six units to the acre; a very desirable plot indeed.

So far nothing at all had been said about it. He knew that Cliff knew that he knew about the ground and the consent, but he was holding back. Why? Until it came into the open and he could see the way the wind was blowing, he was chary of turning down the pig suggestion out of hand. Always ready for a deal; yes, but pigs! He wasn't so sure about that. He'd have to feel his way.

Whether it was the whisky working — he'd had a fair amount — or some other chemical reaction, Lappitt, as he watched Bowles silently puffing away at his pipe and re-settling his leg on the stool, felt his hackles rise as he recalled the farmer's defence of the carpenter when he'd told him to get a move on. What a damn cheek!

This steeled him into facing up to Bowles.

"Even if I agreed to take the pigs, I'd want a lot more than four hundred quid to settle the job. I can't afford to carry forward a loss on the shop job to pig farming, a thing I know nothing about . . . unless. . . ." He hesitated.

"Well, go on then," urged Bowles, interested enough to take the pipe out of his mouth.

Boldly, Sam spat it out, ". . . unless we take that planning consent of yours on the little meader into the reckoning and have an all-round deal: shop — pigs — ground. What d'ye say to that, Cliff?"

Bowles was cagey, though he could see room for manoeuvre in the proposal.

"I don't know about that, Sam. That's a very valuable piece of ground and the agents have been after me. They say they've already got two enquiries, though they're jumpin' the gun a bit since I've not given them the job yet."

Although this news unsettled Sam, making him more

anxious than ever, he kept his cool. Cliff was a difficult man to deal with. It was no good being over-eager. He would have to go through the usual pokerface rigmarole before coming to grips. Draining his glass, he replaced it on the sideboard.

"Anyway, I'll be off now. Think about it, Cliff. I'm sure we can agree a figure for the ground; no need to pay out good money to agents when we can settle it between ourselves."

If Ted thought Lappitt's yard was a shambles before, he certainly noticed no improvement now. He had given in a list of materials required on site and was sent to the yard by the foreman to chase it up when two days elapsed without delivery. He was greatly intrigued when, rounding the corner by the back office, the stink of boiling pig swill assailed his nostrils. There, hard by the plumber's shop, in a kind of alcove hitherto given over to scrap metal and odds and ends, he observed a newly constructed sty containing half a dozen pigs, all Middle Whites. Astonished, he turned to the storeman. "Going into pig farming, are we?"

"Don't talk to me about bloody pigs. He's got me feeding them, boiling up swill morning, noon and night in that old copper in the scullery back of the office. I don't know what the union 'ud say, but you should hear my missus! He'd best stay away from her. Parsley's threatened to let them loose or send for the RSPCA: them pigs is used to free range, you know."

Parsley had been against the whole deal. He told Sam he had been conned into agreeing an inflated price for the ground which would be difficult to square at the bank. Not only that, he had got himself lumbered with the last six of several dozen pigs he knew for a fact Bowlsey had been trying to get rid of even before his accident.

Ted was now working on the local authority housing site where his fastidious treatment of even the most trivial chore, pernickety carcasing and careful floor bashing was having a detrimental effect on the carpentry gang's stage payments. His work stood out like the Post Office tower; it was superb, especially the second fixing finishing which was admired all round; except by his craft mates who grumbled continuously and wanted him shifted elsewhere so that they could return to pay packets laced by the bonus payments to which they had been accustomed.

He displayed total disregard for incentives of any kind, content to do his own thing in the manner which was second nature to him, apparently quite satisfied with basic financial return.

Jock, an outspoken Dundonian who had opted to remain in the South after completing his national service — he'd had to marry a local girl who obstinately refused to move up-country away from her mum — gave it as his opinion that Ted had been born centuries too late, that he would have been a dead cert for serfdom in medieval castle and cathedral construction, and happy as a sandboy with a groat a day and a gallon of ale at the weekends.

One day, as the men entered the shed for the lunch-time break, they found Sloper, the tea boy, in a state of suppressed excitement. As a tea boy, Sloper was the best, for he could be relied on to consistently drum up a brew with body and aroma, a brew that even Lappitt had been known to relish when, on occasion, he dropped in for a word with the foreman and stayed for a mugga.

"What's the matter wiv ya, me ol' cock? What's eatin' ya?" asked the cockney plasterer, a perceptive man whose wife bred Staffordshire bull terriers in West Drayton.

Eagerly, Sloper replied, "It's that carpenter, ain't it.

Mr Perfection. No wonder he's different. D'ye know what?"

"Well, wot then, for god's sake?"

Intent on making the most of it, Sloper paused until he was sure he had their full attention.

"'E's different, ain't 'e? You must 'ave noticed?"

"In me pay packet, that's where I noticed," observed a disgruntled carpenter, sourly.

"'E's supposed to come from Newcastle, but 'e don't talk much like a Georgie, do 'e? 'Course 'e don't — and why? 'Cause 'e's a bleed'n' lord, that's why!"

He stood back to observe the effect of this information and a hush fell on the workers ringing the slow combustion stove.

"Gerroff!" exploded the plasterer, derisively. "What you on about?"

"Jus' what I said! I've found out that 'e's a lord, a belted bleed'n' earl."

"How the hell do you know that?"

Sloper wasn't yet ready to spill the beans entirely. He wanted to savour the impression he had made on the chaps before revealing his sources. It was not often he had their complete attention; now he had them in the palm of his hand.

"Havers! He's nae mare lord than I am."

Sloper turned sharply on Jock, "All right, clever bugger, tell me this then, why does 'e 'ave 'is name sewn inside the inside pocket of 'is jacket: Edward, Lord Blyford?"

"Bloody 'ell," exclaimed one of the labourers, impressed.

This was followed by a lengthy silence, broken at last by the perceptive plasterer.

"An' what would you be doin' lookin' in the inside pocket of 'is jacket? 'Ow many more inside pockets you acquainted with?"

The general attention was immediately diverted to this aspect and a hefty ruddy-visaged labourer solemnly reckoned that instead of six inch nails to hang their clothes on they ought to insist on having lockers, same as factory workers.

"So that's what happened to the fiver I lost last Friday week!" commented another. "I'll not 'ang me togs in 'ere any more."

"Aw, come off it. You know bloody well I'd never pinch off me mates."

Certainly, it has to be said that Sloper was more indignant than embarrassed by the turn of events. While no one thought for a minute he would lift anything, that was not to say he wouldn't stick his nose into anybody's business given the chance.

Ted had been sent over to the farmhouse to fix some new kitchen units and attend to several jobs pending since Bowles' hospitalisation, the farmer having waxed enthusiastically to his wife about "this marvellous carpenter" whose services he recommended they take advantage of while still available, judging that such excellence could not long be sustained within the House of Lappitt.

When he arrived back on site a few days later, Ted found the new deferential attitude difficult to fathom. He was quite used to the carpenters moaning about his precision and geeing him up when they were within shooting distance of a bonus target, but on the whole had got on quite well with the chaps who clearly accepted him within the fraternity, giving him full marks as an interesting commentator on social and political affairs, and one who handled Sam Lappitt with easy good manners and aplomb. So he was at a loss to explain why this feeling of change in their association now kept on cropping up.

Even at the digs a variation in temperature was

evident; a shift in the climate of B&B relationship. For instance, hitherto the daughter of the house, a good looking girl in her late teens, recently released from high school and hopeful to be teacher trained, had given him hands off signals with pert, toss-of-the-head monition. Not, mind you, that he had made advances of any kind, for in that department he was inclined to be backward, but his distant admiration had been noted and development discouraged.

Now she was all over him! Even asking him out to the pictures, and was dead set on arranging a picnic to Christmas Common at the coming holiday weekend.

What the hell's going on, thinks Ted, recalling the increased consideration and respect that had been his lot since his return on site from the farmhouse job.

He was not ass enough to lap it up without questioning, and although he enjoyed holding hands and all the rest of it — in and out of the cinema — he couldn't but wonder what had triggered the change in attitude.

Ted's landlady was sister-in-law to one of the bricklayers on the council site so it was not difficult to see how Sloper's bit of inside information might have percolated the system. On the other hand, it was not altogether unlikely that the landlady had indulged her own means of access to first hand information.

Be that as it may, what with one thing and another, Ted made up his mind to get to the bottom of it. At the first opportunity he would confront the men in the shed.

Meanwhile, back at HQ, Lappitt was finding himself in deep water. The bank manager had been in touch with regional office about the application for increased facilities to substantially cover the cost of the land to be acquired from Bowles. First soundings gave little scope for optimism.

Not for the first time, a detailed account of works in

progress was called for, with cash flow projection for twelve months ahead.

This, Sam considered to be a bad sign, and he could forsee that burning the midnight oil was likely to become a regular feature in preparing the required information and wrestling with the complications of concocting an optimistic prognosis.

He was not very good at it, in fact dreaded the paperwork involved. The last time it happened, he recalled with chagrin, the bank's regional office shot him down in flames when the figures didn't tally, concluding that his forecasts sounded more like Wimpey International than Lappitt (Pickstock) Ltd.

This was one area where he had to go it alone come what may, for Parsley Jack's post office savings account could throw very little light on the intricacies of high finance. Resident carpenter and confidant, Parsley was in and out of the office a dozen times a day, but his efforts, though sympathetic, were of little use for the task in hand. And Old Eagle Eye, who was the accounts department, though quite good at costing up the jobs and fiddling about with his double entries, panicked when asked to deal with anything else, pleading that doctoring the works in progress or manipulating cash flow was quite beyond his ken.

Nevertheless, by dint of burning the candle at both ends, the figures were eventually produced and delivered to the bank in fear and trembling.

What had made matters seem much worse to Lappitt was that at the back of his mind he dreaded the thumbs down from the bank because, in a rare moment of bravado, he had sealed the arrangement by shaking hands with Bowles. After all, had it not been *his* idea to have a three-way deal? two parts of which — the livestock and the shop job — had already been implemented. What Bowlsey would have to say if the money couldn't be found constituted a recurring nightmare.

As if this were not enough tribulation, one of the neighbours complained to the police about the pig smells wafting continually through his house — "smell pollution of the environment", he called it. Then the whole thing really escalated when another townsman went to the council, causing the sanitary inspector to call round at the yard to read the riot act.

Sam was informed that pigs could only be kept at a certain distance from residential or business property, and that the sanitary conditions in the yard were not acceptable, also that the occupants of the sty must be evacuated to some more suitable place before the local rat population got wind of the new gravy bowl — if, indeed, they hadn't already done so.

Actually, they *had* done so, and the first thing each morning the storeman would remove the unfortunates and reset the traps, grumbling to Lappitt that such employment was outside his contractual obligations and forcing the builder to give him a weekly back-hander.

Eventually, at the instigation of Parsley, Lappitt cut his losses and sent the pigs to market without reserve. In his eyes the outcome did nothing to enhance the name of Bowles, for he discovered too late that the bottom had fallen out of the pig market even before he had taken the plunge.

Watched intently by Joby, Sloper was busying himself with pre-luncheon preparations. He had boiled the water ready for drumming-up, emptied into it a quarter of the finest Ceylon, stirring thoroughly with a length of tile batten, and temporarily replaced the tea bucket on top of the stove with Joby's immaculate though well-worn shovel. Within a few minutes an air of culinary well-being permeated the shed, the effluvia of the strong brew vying with spitting and sizzling streaky rashers for nasal appreciation.

Joby, ex-county council roadman, had a year or two before come in from the cold, Lappitt taking him on because, at the time, he was short of labourers and looked kindly on any man used to working without supervision. Joby's rheumatics, the result of thirty years' surfeit of fresh air tending banks and verges, drains and ditches in all weathers, had improved for a while, but he had been off sick again with his chest, and when he returned, the foreman, an understanding man, allowed him to knock-off early to relish from a pew as near the stove as possible the comparative comfort of the shed; sympathetically recalling that the poor old fellow lived on his own in an isolated roadman's cottage which, in its austerity, was more like an eighteenth-century but and ben than a council property.

Joby maintained that a shovel fry-up was vastly superior to the conventional kind and, in support of this, would retail that he had once known a man who worked in the kitchens at the Ritz and who had no hesitation in endorsing this opinion.

Of course, as far as Sloper was concerned, it was not all brotherly love. He had an understanding with the chaps that when it came to providing meals he expected to be more than reimbursed; which meant, in effect, that they kept him in cigarettes.

This, then, was the scene that confronted Ted when, entering the shed, he took off his jacket and hung it on a nail.

Sloper was in expansive form.

"Mornin', your lordship!"

"Mornin', Slopah!" responded Ted, latching on to the mood.

"I trusts I finds you well this mornin', m'lord?"

"In fine fettle, Slopah, fine fettle."

Shovel fry-up in the shed

"An' how would you prefer your bacon this mornin', m'lord?"

"Need you ask, Slopah? Done to a frazzle, man, done to a frazzle."

Joby interjected, "I met a lord once when I was in the army. Near Nijmegen it was. As nice a fella as you would wish to meet. He was only a sub'ton."

Sloper raised his eyebrows.

"No need to go continental, Joby, when we got our very own lordship 'ere and now." He paused, then, in the grand manner, "Edward, my Lord Blyford, allow me to introduce you. Lord Blyford, this 'ere's Joby."

Ted stared incredulously.

"Where on earth did you get that from?"

Without a word, Sloper went to the coat rail, opened Ted's jacket and revealed the tag.

This sent Ted into fits of laughter. Rocking to and fro, he slapped his thighs with the flat of his hands.

"So that's what it's all about. Well, I'll be damned! Exposed by a tailor's tag!"

The shed door opened noisily.

"What's this, then? Where's the comic?" It was Lappitt. He was cock-a-hoop, having come straight from the bank where the manager had given him the nod — unofficially, of course — that he now awaited optimistically confirmation of the regional office decision.

"We was only 'avin' a laugh, guv'nor." Sloper would address Lappitt as "Mr Lappitt", "Sam", "guv'nor" or "guv" in turn, according to circumstances, having a nice feel for the occasion and highly sensitised to his boss's current metabolism.

Without more ado, Sam sat down and, turning to Ted, said "Got your note. You're not serious?"

"'Fraid so, Mr Lappitt." Here, he looked at Soper who, ears pricked, was fussing around the boss with a steaming mugga.

"Been summoned to the ancestral home. Duty calls."

"Oh? What's that mean?"

"An interesting situation has cropped up."

Making sure that Sloper was out of earshot, Lappitt suggested eagerly, "I could spring another penny or two if it's a question of rate?"

It wasn't.

As the men filed in for the break, Lappitt took himself off and Sloper, anxious to be the first with the news, called out to whom it might concern, "Ted's leavin'!"

The relief of the chippies was comical to behold — immediate and very obvious. They were a bunch not generally given to displaying emotion, but suddenly they found Ted to be an exceedingly fine fellow, slapping him on the back, shouldering him and ruffling his hair while expressing sorrow at losing such a great exponent of the joinery art. There was no doubt he would be "sorely missed", "difficult to replace" — his departure "mourned by all".

"Here, hang on! hang on!" expostulated Ted. "I'm not dead yet, you know. I'm going back home to work, not to be buried."

So they complimented him on his sense of humour, for always seeing the funny side and, after another round of back-slapping, insisted he should have first choice of the shovel rashers.

The girl at the digs must have grown genuinely fond of him because, even after he explained away his mother's elocutionary predilections to a lifetime spent in domestic service with gentlefolk in general, and Lord Blyford's family in particular — where else would he have got the hand-me-down togs? — she nevertheless resolved to obtain a transfer application to a Newcastle teacher training college, so that when Ted took up his new appointment as Head of Carpentry within the building section at the technical school, they would be able to bring their courtship to proper fruition.

Yes, he did get the teaching job in the end, but only after it had been offered and rejected in turn by both the other short-listed candidates who, he calculated, must have had the chance of preferred situations.

As he said goodbye to Pickstock, the last thing he saw and heard, down by the station approach, was the old woman in the Marie Lloyd hat, still urging all and sundry to count their blessings.

Beautiful as a Butterfly

HIS brother's son, Alec, had been missing for the second day and Thomson was more than annoyed. Being late for work was one thing, but when it came to being absent without leave it wasn't funny, especially since he had become dependent on his nephew for the smooth, day-to-day running of the office and yard; had in fact, over the last year or two, come to lean on him increasingly in this respect.

Thomson's brother, Sid, several years his senior, had once again come to the office to check if his lad — he was almost twenty six! — had turned up or been in touch.

The brothers faced each other across the desk.

"It fair beats me!" declared Sid, rolling another cigarette and licking the Woodbine paper carefully before lighting up.

Thomson, glum, said nothing. For the umpteenth time he wondered what in the name of Satan Alec was up to. But, peculiarly, mostly he was thinking of Sid.

It took an emergency for Sid to visit him. Normally, he never came near. For years Whealer had employed him as a builder's labourer. He could turn his hand to anything, was more generally skilled than most fully-fledged craftsmen. Certainly, he had the reputation of being the best outdoor all-rounder in Pickstock.

Ever since they were boys, Thomson had worried about him. Now, when he considered his own personal circumstances — the splendid new car standing outside the office, his fine house and settled family life — then thought of Sid, his stomach turned over.

All his life he had wanted Sid, willed him, to be better

off than himself, because somehow he felt that was how it should be. He was well-balanced and mature, except perhaps when it came to "getting on". It intrigued the younger brother how, despite appearances, Sid was the better man: he knew it and Sid knew it. Sid could use his hands and his brains when he wanted, had the capacity to enjoy himself and was good company when he chose, yet his wife had left him when she realised he was never going to be anything more than a builder's labourer. And, by the lights of most people, she was right!

At the time, Sid argued, "All right! I'm only a labourer, but I like my work, and I am the best — ask anybody in the trade", adding, pointedly, "If I'd known it was a masterman you were after. I'd've had a word with me brother". But it was no use. She'd set her heart on joining the middle class, being so thoroughly indoctrinated that she even swapped their single leaf lavatory seat for a double flap, which Sid considered the ultimate snobbery. As it turned out, long before she threw in the towel she had her sights on a salaried replacement with prospects. But that was all history now.

For fully five minutes the two men sat without speaking, weighing each other up and cogitating. It was a happy release when at last the phone rang and there was Alec at the other end saying he would be back in the office after lunch and would explain everything then. When his father, blustering, snatched the phone from Thomson's hand and started an argument, Alec simply hung up and left him to his paddy.

Thomson's only comment was, "'Bout time he got married and settled down," at which Sid picked up his cap off the desk and marched out of the office, banging the door behind him, leaving his brother wondering what he'd said wrong.

Alec never did adequately explain his absenteeism; merely, as an excuse, used the tellyscript mumbo-jumbo, "I felt I had to get away for a couple of days to sort myself out."

Of course, Thomson guessed there was a girl in it somewhere, but diplomatically decided to keep quiet and let nature take its course. As far as he was concerned it was sufficient that Alec was back in harness and, although he seemed preoccupied, it was probably nothing that a bit of the old grindstone wouldn't put right.

As everybody knows, when there's a recession one can't pick and choose, can only try for such jobs as are being touted around. Now, for the first time in years, Thomson did not have one house under construction on land of his own.

Apart from bread-and-butter local authority housing and the clearing up of sundry contract works, all he had in front was some maintenance at a papermill up river, the building of several pairs of flint cottages with pigsties to match for a Chiltern gentleman farmer, and a new public house on a plot he had himself reluctantly sold to an out-of-town free house speculator when the local brewery considered the asking price too much.

So, when the manager of the mill phoned to say he had another job lined up, he was quite pleased until he found that it was demolition work: they wanted a ninety foot chimney taken down and the rubble disposed of.

His first reaction was to curse his condition. Here was a potential windfall of first rate brick rubble and he had nowhere to place it. Would, in fact, have to hawk around to see if some other builder could find a home for it. Another thing, before beginning he would have to do his homework, for he had never before demolished an industrial chimney.

In the last couple of years he had encouraged Alec to extend his knowledge of estimating by pricing up most of the smaller jobs. Now, he decided to involve his nephew on site development, at least to the extent that office work allowed, reasoning that if he could keep him at stretch with a bit more in his pocket, he might be less inclined to absenteeism.

When they drove out together to have a look at the chimney, Alec, eager to earn his spurs, made a suggestion.

"We could fall it across that strip of land above the river bank over there."

Thomson demured. "Only a few degrees off line and it 'ud be in the river. The Thames Conservancy wouldn't like that. We'd have a bore flooding the countryside for miles around." He paused. "Trouble is, they want it done pronto, and just at the moment that poses a difficulty, for we must have someone who knows what he's doing."

The gentleman farmer's architect was a pernickety creature, though otherwise quite a reasonable chap as architects go. The firm had never done a flint job before and a number of mistakes were made; like knapping the flints on the scaffold instead of on the ground, so that not only time but temper was expended when the brickies ran into a load rotten at the core. Then there was trouble with one or two of the chaps refusing to wear the protective goggles now prescribed as a must when knapping.

Thomson had the lorry scouring the countryside, visiting all the chalk pits for miles around, and the result was a mixed bag that took a lot of sorting out, nibbling away at the percentage of profit which contained more than an element of guesswork.

The pub job turned out to be a pain in the neck too because the architect, convinced that Thomson had asked and got far too much for the ground, determined to claw back as much as possible under the building contract; this, though the negotiations for the plot had been nothing to do with him. But he'd always had the reputation of being a man keen for more than his pound of flesh.

All in all "a bleak prospect", as Thomson put it when running through the work programme with Alec.

The men in the shed on the council site sat around the stove eating, drinking and smoking while eyeing Twiggy with new interest. Many considered him a cut above the rest, not because his father was on the town council, but because, when he peed he always did it in the sentrybox privvy, and could be relied on to aim clear of the piece of four by two that served as a seat; whereas, especially if it was anything other than a housing site they were working on, they relieved themselves urinally anywhere that suited.

Yes, Jeffrey Branch was one on his own, but what engaged the corporate attention currently was his matrimonial prospects.

During the week, news had leaked that he was all set for tying up with Janie Pennington, whose widowed father had died six months before, leaving her a sweet and tobacconist business in the town, a splendid little shop with a flat over the top. Only that morning the local paper had confirmed the leak by carrying an announcement in the engagement column to the effect that a match had been arranged.

There ensued the usual noisy banter.

"'E won't want to be seen out wi' us lot Friday nights at the *Wheatsheaf*, any more, will 'e?"

"When you movin' in, Twig?" enquired Ron, only for Tabby, his mate to counter immediately, "Movin' in? You must be jokin'! 'E's bin 'avin' 'is sweet ration for months, 'aven't yer, Twig?"

Ingratiatingly, Will said, "Always did think 'e 'ad the makin's of a gentleman, wot wi' 'is fine ways an' finicky 'abits."

"There's nae accountin' fur taste," lamented the Scots carpenter dolefully, shaking his head while examining Twiggy up and down with critical eyes. His was a special interest because he lived two doors away from the shop and had been friendly with Janie's father, sharing his radical taste in politics.

Alfie, never seen without a fag or a pipe in his mouth, was thinking ahead.

"No need to go toutin' round no more. We'll all get our cigs and baccy at discount rates — Twiggy'll see to that."

The object of this rare attention, complete with comfortable, self-satisfied grin on his face, let them get on with it, pleased to be the centre of attention for once, though not in any way as confident of what lay ahead as his mates seemed to be. The fact was that the notice in the paper had come as more of a shock to him than a surprise to them. He had certainly not been consulted about its insertion, true though it was that in the last few days Janie had been making up to him more than usual.

Their courtship — if courtship be the right word — had been punctuated by cooling-off periods due almost entirely to Janie back-pedalling when Jeffrey displayed a touch more than his usual tepid enthusiasm, though she was quick enough to fan the embers when she felt like it.

"She's only making use of you", his father had warned discerningly. The trouble was that she was not only too clever for him, but had reserves of emotion quite beyond his grasp.

When they strolled down the high street together, he would be concerned that she attracted keen attention from wayout likely lads on the prowl. Once, referring to her colourful, skin-tight togs and brilliant hairstyling, Twiggy, solicitous and anxious, suggested: "Why don't you unpretty yourself, my lovely, then you wouldn't have to bother 'bout them wolf whistles and cat callers?" Of course, as usual, he was on the wrong track. She only feigned annoyance: admiration was bread, butter and jam to her.

But an ad in the paper! That was county custom, something to be expected from the toffee-nosed set, and quite foreign to the likes of him. Janie was known for being precise in everything she did, but this really was taking it a bit far . . . and it wasn't as if it was tucked away in some corner of the paper, either. It had the distinction of being the only item under the "Engagements" heading.

Twiggy accepted ragging by the chaps more as a token of mateyness than anything else. A plasterer by trade, he was exceptionally good looking and dressed well off site, but, some thought, lacked a bit on top. Certainly, at times he was easily led, and gullible in discourse to the point of taking hearsay as gospel.

"You wouldn't believe this, Twig," Tabby confided, "but I could have sworn last night I see Janie's name up in lights yonder outside the community hall: 'Janie Pennington in Getting Married'."

"Go on!"

Wide-eyed, he let this intelligence sink in, then responded, "She's bin in the Pickstock Players since high school, and I know she's rehearsing a new play. She don't usually get the best parts, but she's keen. Tried to get me to join, but I wasn't any good — or so the boss man said."

"Aw, what a shame!" Tabby sympathised, winking at Ron. Then, staunchly, "I'm sure you would have bin champion, Twig. . . ."

Ron, lying flat on his back on a scaffold board

propped up with flettons, looked dreamily at the rustic corrugations of the tin roof of the shed.

"She's a smasher, is Janie, a real smasher. A mettlesome filly, I'd say. That's what bothers me. Are you sure you're gonna be able to handle her, Twig?"

Twiggy grinned sheepishly, but did not reply.

"Do you think he's man enough for her, Tabby?"

"That's a real puzzling question, that is, Ron. It all depends on 'is chemical make-up. I read all about it once in a woman's magazine. There's big, brawny blokes that are bloody useless in bed, and there's little, scraggy buggers that can't get enough. You must 'ave seen them up the high street walking along wi' real nice birds, and y' think to yerself, 'Wot in 'eavens name can she see in 'im'?"

His recollecting juices in full flow, eagerly he said, "Did I ever tell you 'bout this bird I picked up in Maidenhead?"

Meanwhile, over on the other side of the stove, Harry, the failed university man from Aylesbury — a dyed-in-the-wool socialist, he boasted of being a reasonable fanatic — had started another of his exploratory discussions, this time with Mick, an occasional Catholic who, in support of his beliefs, had been desperately trying to recall something significant from his catechismic upbringing.

Mick was saying, ". . . I don't get you, Harry. You're an intelligent man, yet you don't accept anything in the Bible, or give the Church credit where credit is due. . ." Here, dropping his voice and speaking defensively, he divulged, "I've had prayers answered, 'cos I have faith." Then, raising his voice again, ". . . and I'm not ashamed of it!"

To his surprise, Harry responded encouragingly.

"Quite right, too. It's not everybody's got faith, not one in a thousand, I'd say. But we're all born with a certain amount of intelligence, ain't we? Are we to use it or not? Faith, we're told, is beyond reason, so it's an implant. I wish I had it, I genuinely wish I had it. It would make life comprehensible, outlook hopeful. But all I've got is a little intelligence to use as best as I can, and hope that maybe one day I, too, may somehow qualify for the implant. You don't know how lucky you are with your faith."

A silence came between them and both appeared deep in thought, Mick displaying a kind of superior look of satisfaction, until a mischievous grin spread across Harry's face.

"How 'bout leaving it to me in your will, Mick? Or, better still, you could have a message sewn into your inside jacket pocket 'case you get knocked over — same as folks do who leave their corneas or kidneys or other unmentionable private parts to poor buggers wot ain't got any: 'I bequeath my faith to Harry of Aylesbury in recognition of his stimulating conversation and thought-provoking tutorials in the site mess shed at Pickstock'. Eh? How 'bout it?"

Pleased with his whimsy, he laughed raucously, almost falling backwards off the bench.

Mick was patently uneasy.

"That's blasphemy. You and I, we're poles apart." Then, suddenly aggressive, he retaliated, "Anyway, I don't care what you say; you're only jealous. I've got me faith, that's all that matters, and I'll take it with me to the grave, thank you very much!"

"And of course, you'll expect to go to heaven, to be met by St Peter at the Pearly Gates, and welcomed by the Holy Ghost to the sound of trumpets?"

"Yes . . . well . . . I believe in the hereafter, don't I? I'll be reunited with my family and my ancestors."

Harry's eyebrows elevated as incredulity surfaced.

"The presumption of the man! The sheer bloody

effrontery! What makes you think you're so special? What grounds have you for supposing this poxy race of ours deserves anything better than oblivion?"

He searched Mick's face for a glimmer of reaction.

Stabbing the air with an index finger, Harry scoffed, "Let me tell you, sonny boy, nobody's going to hold out the friendly mit, there's no room at the inn. There's no bloody inn!"

Grim as a first year undertaker's apprentice, Mick opened his mouth to retort, when, "Wot you two natt'rin on about?"

Butting in was Dave, Mick's mate, who hitherto had been employing full powers of concentration in stuffing as much bread and cheese into his mouth as it was possible to do without choking. Now, ready for afters, he was opening a little square cardboard box from which he lifted a Joe Lyon's apple tart.

Mick turned to him and said, "It's only cleverdick showing his ignorance. . ."

At that moment the shed door creaked open, dithering on its hinges, and in stalked the foreman.

"Ain't you lot got no soddin' work to go to? Or would you *prefer* the dole? Want me to crack the soddin' whip all the time like a soddin' sergeant-major, don't yer?" Sad-faced, he looked down at them with mock appeal.

"Bloody slave driver!" Tabby snorted, nevertheless getting to his feet, as did the rest.

Bill Sodder was by nature a melancholy man, and one not to be trifled with, though, as far as anyone knew, oblivious of the nickname applied to him by one and all.

When confronting a man in argument or anger, he would squint twenty degrees off centre, as if spieling from an autocue, only in the last moment of coming to the point refocusing on target. This flummoxed many to the extent that they would avoid further palaver, unable to dispel the feeling that they had been caught with their trousers down.

He had never been bedevilled by the desire to be all things to all men and, though at heart a born martinet, was experienced enough to know when to unbend a little, to relax, to give a bit for the sake of labour relations, just so long as it wasn't too much, and didn't cost anything.

"Come on, then, let's be 'avin' ya! And you, Branch, you're wanted at the office."

"Wot, me?"

"Name's Branch, ain't it?"

"Wot they want me for?"

"How the hell should I know."

Knowing the office was shut for the lunch hour, Twiggy stayed behind as the men filed out in the wake of Sodder. To fortify his punctured morale, the plasterer helped himself to another mugga from the dregs in the tea bucket and sat down, tortured by conjecture on the possible ways in which he might have transgressed the Thomson code. But not for long. . . .

His thoughts turned to Janie and the advert in the paper, and panic seized him. Now it had come to the crunch, he was not at all certain he wanted to get married. She had kept him dangling so long that somehow he had given up thinking about her that way. He would, of course, be more than happy to take her to the cinema, or go for a walk by the river, but his dad was probably right when he reckoned he was too young to get wed, wasn't ready for it.

It quite overwhelmed him when he thought of the responsibilities that lay ahead, and anyway, he didn't need Tabby to tell him that he wasn't one of those maleish males who could hardly wait. . . . Sitting there in the shed he suddenly felt hemmed in, caged, and soon found himself listening in a daze to what was going on outside, picking out the sounds and visualising the movements of men and materials.

As he rubbed the toe of his boot speculatively into the dirt floor, he was conscious of the clang and clamour the bricklayers made clipping the flettons with the edge of the trowel for bats and closures, tapping them into place on course, scraping off the excess mortar; or scraping the pug off the mortar boards while holding a brick poised in the left hand — all, that is, except Freddie, who did it the other way round and so was generally left to work on his own.

Being a council site, the bricks were flettons, including the facings, which was just as well, because it made it a little bit more difficult to distinguish the men from the boys. In the mind's eye Twig followed the scaffolder's progress as he dropped the boards on to the putlogs on the second lift of the fourth pair, and securely locked-in the fittings with the little tool that looked just like the one he used at home to tighten the bed springs. On the third pair, the carpenters were shoving the ceiling joists across the inside walls and he recognised the dull dong as the lengths of three by two bounced off the brickwork.

At the back of the foreman's office, the plumber was laboriously using a hacksaw on a length of galvanised tube, but the loudest noise of all came from the first pair where Billy Boy was causing general hilarity as, striding up and down the ladder on to the scaffold, he regaled the men with detailed descriptions of his love life with Rosie, his latest heart-throb.

Suddenly, reverie was rudely shattered when, close by, Sodder was heard bellowing at Billy. In a trice, Twig grabbed hold of his jacket, left the shed and, mounting his bike, pedalled smartly off in the direction of the high street.

For a certainty, had the occasion demanded, the cub reporter on the *Pickstock Courier* would have described Janie Pennington as a vivacious redhead, and for once he would have been right, except for the understatement.

She was the sort of girl who caused heads to swivel as, moving with model deportment, she navigated precinct or pavement, more often than not leaving a litter of casualties; like chaps walking into lamp-posts, or women falling over other peoples' prams; yes, even the women, which must be the greater compliment. It wasn't that she had sticky-up, rainbow-coloured hair — bright chestnut it was, shiny as a newly shucked conker.

Her father had kept her on a very tight rein, so, remarkably, Janie's experience of the opposite sex had been confined to one or two scuffles with such as Jeffrey Branch, himself a milk-and-water exponent of the art of mixed all-in wrestling, and with whom she had originally come into contact only because both their dads were on the town council.

Alec she met when he called at the flat in response to her request for an estimate for painting and sundry minor building work to the shop property which was sorely in need of attention, father having neglected it in his later years.

They got on well and in no time at all graduated from dallying to dating, one thing leading to another until, one day, greatly daring, they fixed up to spend the night at an ancient hostelry in Chiltern country, situated a discreet distance from Pickstock.

After a golden evening holding hands while sauntering through the moonlit hotel grounds — a romantic interlude the like of which neither had tasted before — Alec was beside himself with passionate intent.

Alas, the prelims were more fruitful than the consummation.

Here, it is necessary to draw a veil over the proceedings and advance our recording to the morning after, though, in all fairness, it can be confirmed that they did sleep together — soundly.

Picture a double bed in an old-fashioned timbered room, complete with the usual appurtenances: the whole thing so far a nightmare! She eager and willing, he, finding it quite impossible to come out of his shell, hardly able to put a foot right; so far, even attempts at discourse impotent.

First light merged into glorious morn, and responding to her wish, Alec rose to open the curtains.

As Janie emerged from the shadows and turned her head on the pillow, the sun god struck, glossing the thick silky hair with a dazzling brilliance. Stunned, Alec gaped at her, mouth ajar.

"You must be the most beautiful girl in . . . er . . . Pickstock," he stammered, quickly getting back into bed.

Patently offended by this bungling attempt at compliment, she upbraided, "In Pickstock! It's not a very big place, is it?"

"Well, England then."

"Oh, yeah? The usual phrase is 'the most beautiful girl in the world'. There's no charge for, no disadvantage in exaggerating as far as lovemaking overtures are concerned. It's expected."

Sulkily, he responded, "Sorry I don't match up to your expectations."

"Not had much of a chance finding out, have we? Strikes me, you're even more of a novice than I am, and that's saying something. And here's me thinking you a man of the world about to sweep me off my feet!" She was now intent on speaking her mind. "Ever been with a girl before? Or is it that as soon as we're all set for the nitty gritty, you find me unattractive?"

"Oh no! You mustn't think that. I think you're lovely, really I do. It's just that I'm a bit . . . well . . . overwhelmed. To tell you the truth, if you were less attractive, had, say, just a good figure, or fine legs, or a beautiful face, or lovely hair, or . . . or just one of these, I'm sure I'd be perfectly all right. But you've got the lot . . . in fact. . . ." he hesitated.

"Keep going — you're doing very nicely," she encouraged.

"I was going to say, it's your very perfection that's your biggest drawback." He paused, then, almost with humility, conceded, "It beats me what you see in me."

She smiled radiantly, pleased with the result of her goading.

"That's much better! You see, you can do it if you try. At least, the talking parts." She frowned. "The performance . . . well . . . it's supposed to follow. If only you were a bit better on the practical side, you could soon get your act together. Anyway, a step in the right direction," she concluded.

She became pensive again, and absentmindedly twirled his hair so that a strand stuck up above his forehead like a marlin spike.

"I don't see what I see in you, either," she reflected, "but that's not the point, is it? You were talking about me."

There followed another silence. By now he was lying back on the pillow, eyes closed and day dreaming. Elevating herself on an elbow, with a forefinger she drew a line down the bridge of his nose, repeating the movement until, tentatively, she said, "It's not very . . . um . . . it's rather small, isn't it?"

Embarrassed, he opened his eyes.

"If it is, it's only because it's hardly been . . . hardly. . . It's in good shape, anyway, whatever you think."

"Whatever are you rabbiting on about?"

"It's not easy to explain. . . ."

She flopped back on the pillow, laughing.

"You're such a fool! But just the same I quite like you . . . could get very fond of you. Innocence is your best feature." She stroked his nose again and consoled, "It doesn't really matter, so long as it's in good working order when the time comes . . . when . . . you have a cold in the head . . . or something."

"Eh?"

He looked extremely puzzled. Still, he had to admit that she had taken it all rather well in the circumstances. Soon they would be up and about, the whole thing just a nagging memory.

"Some people have built-in experience. Others have to work at it. Don't you think so, Alec?"

He grunted non-committally.

"Take me. On the face of it I am as inexperienced as you are. But there's very little to learn when you come to think of it, is there? It's just a matter of pointing yourself in the right direction and letting nature take over."

He was looking very serious.

"I've been too busy earning a living, I suppose. Some people can cram a lot into half an hour on the back seat of a car. Others, like me, take time to get acclimatised." Then, fiercely, defensively, he said, "That's not to say when the time comes I'll be any the worse at it."

"Ah, yes . . . when the time comes. . . ." she intoned, gravely.

He turned to look at her. There was no doubt about it, she was most intelligent, and exceptionally female.

He bestirred himself. All might have been well if he had not tried that last desperate sortee, a bit of strong arm stuff which fizzled out when, unfortunately, he rolled right over her and fell out of bed on the other side, taking the bed clothes with him as he landed on the floor with a thump that rattled the bits and pieces on the dressing table.

"That settles it," declared Janie. "I'm getting dressed and I'm clearing out as soon as I've had my breakfast."

"Chaucer was one of us. Did you know that, Mick?"

"You mean the Canterbury Tales bloke, the Pilgrim's Way and all that?"

"The same."

"Gerroff!"

"He was clerk of the works at the Tower of London, and foreman of a job not far from here, St George's Chapel, Windsor."

"No! Is that a fact?"

"Well, you sure live and learn, don't yer," commented Ron.

Harry of Aylesbury was holding court in the Nissen. Nothing he liked better than to air his knowledge, and the inmates of the shed were not averse to a history lesson, particularly when it touched on the building trade. It made a change from the eternal argument about frog up or frog down.

At Thomson's behest, Bill Sodder had gone off somewhere to weigh up a nuisance job, so naturally enough the lunchtime natter had expanded beyond its alloted span, though even before Geoff Chaucer was pitchforked into the arena Harry had been rummaging amongst his anecdotal bric-a-brac to indulge the chaps and enhance the shining hour.

"And mentioning St George's Chapel," he continued, "did you know that when Charles the First was beheaded, the executioner was so nervous he had to have two goes at it? Almost missed completely with the first swing of the axe. Chipped off the king's chin clean as a whistle, complete with half his beard. Of course, Charles had only himself to blame, bloody fool! — put the poor bloke off his stroke by insisting on being executed face up."

"Well I never," exclaimed Willy mildly, "some folk have no consideration for others."

"Yes, and not long ago Charles' tomb in St George's Chapel was opened up so's the splintered bone could be restored to its rightful owner. Not many people know that! Been in possession of the same family ever since the execution. It took three hundred years for someone to do the decent thing and have it buried with the rest of him."

"How'd you come to know 'bout all this," queried Tabby.

"Knew a painter — name of Hughes, came from Slough — he done a lot of decorating in the kitchens at Windsor Castle, he told me."

There was a lengthy pause while the chaps digested this surprising bit of information, some of them stunned by the picture of the executioner wielding an unprofessional axe over the supine figure of the king. No wonder Charles became something of a martyr in the popular imagination!

"And I'll tell you something else, Ben Johnson you know, Willie Shakespeare's mate — he was a tradesman, a bricklayer — worked on Lincoln's Inn. What d'ye think of that?"

Proud of his knowledge and connection with the famous, however fragile, Harry glanced around, intent on measuring the impression his disclosures had made.

Alfie, who had been busy with his own thoughts, was not in the least concerned about Chaucer, King Charles or Ben Johnson. Quite suddenly, as if he had just solved a thorny problem, he burst out, "Only way to take it down is the way the Romans done it."

Several pairs of eyes refocused in his direction.

"Whit y' haverin' aboot?" demanded the Scots carpenter.

"That chimney we gotta take down . . . you know? You must have heard of the Roman method. . . ."

"We've all heard of the French method," Tabby sniggered.

"What you on about?" intervened a voice from the back of the stove.

"Well," explained Alfie, "when the Romans wanted to demolish a building, they'd cut down some trees, stick the boles in a kind of oven, make holes at ground level all round the building, bung the dried-out boles into the holes and turn the hoses on them. The trees expanded, and bob's yer uncle."

They stared at him.

"They didn't have no hose in them days," clever Harry quietly pointed out.

"Well, anyway, they saturated the timber, didn't they? Then, hey presto! the building collapsed. They got it to a fine art, could guarantee to within two degrees which way the pile 'ud fall."

"Oh dear, oh dear!" sighed Will, lighting a fag. "First we get a lecture on King Charles' chinbone, now it's how the Romans went about fallin' a bleedin' chimley. What next?"

"Well, Alfie," Tabby said pointedly, "you're too bloody late wi' yer Roman method, 'cos I happen to know the job's gonna be done by Sid Thomson at the weekend. And 'nother thing, I happen to know, 'e'll not be wantin' any tree trunks or ovens, 'cos he'll do it all off ladders, same as 'e done before at Jackmans, pushing the rubble into the chimney. Seen him do that at Perrins Mill as well, years ago. No need for steeplejacks when Sid's around."

"That's a funny howd'ya-do!" commented Will. "Always thought Thomson and Sid didn't hit it off?"

Surprisingly, Twiggy had something to say.

"I happen to know it was young Alec made the

arrangement."

"Since when you bin privvy to what goes on at the office?"

Twiggy bristled, fixing Will with a steady gaze.

"I was sent for the other day, wasn't I? Alec wanted me to do a little job on Saturday morning, didn't 'e? He just happened to mention the chimney, said he was going to help his dad with it over the weekend."

Which was right enough, except *that* wasn't all Alec had mentioned.

Like everybody else, he had seen the announcement in the paper, so the real reason he had sent for Twig was to test the temperature. He had already concluded that the ad had been inserted by Janie, probably in a fit of pique following their abortive get-together. And he wasn't far wrong at that.

What he didn't know was that Twig had called at the sweet shop on the way to the office to find out what it was all about. *She* did a U-turn, threw herself on his charity, asked his forgiveness, appealed to his better nature. No sooner had the announcement appeared in cold print than she got cold feet, realising what a fool she'd been.

She needn't have bothered, because, scarcely had she begun her plea when Jeffrey, getting the drift for once and expelling an audible sigh of relief, willingly gave up all claim to her person, breach of promise thankfully waived. It was a happy release for the pair of them and they toasted the future with a glass of lemonade.

Fishing for information, Alec had, in the first place, proffered congratulations, and immediately it became only too apparent that the plasterer was off the boil (if, indeed, he had ever been on it), soon letting it out of the bag that the engagement by joint consent had been declared null and void.

Alec was cockahoop, now believing himself to be the only remaining candidate for Janie's affections — hadn't she confessed that she could become quite fond of him? — and confident that, given another opportunity, he could show what he was made of. He would swoop in and corner the market.

Everybody in the know fully expected Janie to eventually choose between Jeffrey and Alec. But her disappointment with both suitors rankled.

So what happened?

Off she went, and without more ado married a Basingstoke butcher — bow-legged, florid, almost a midget — who chanced into her shop one day to buy a box of matches. A complete extrovert of a man with a zest for living, he carried her off to the altar, put a manager into his butcher shop and moved into the flat above the sweet and tobacconist.

There was, as the Scots carpenter put it, "nae accountin' f'r taste". It was he who broke the news to the men in the shed.

"It's no possible," he reflected sadly, "but it's a fact!"

The Sound Barrier

SPECIFICATION in hand and plan on desk, Thomson had been teasing out the architectural ramifications of Mrs Arbuthnot's new house until they formed in his mind a satisfactory whole. He could see it would be an awkward job, calling as it did for lots of purpose-made joinery, intricate plumbing, high standard decoration; he would have to employ his best bricklayers, for the external angles, quoins and arches were legion. And he was not too keen on the architect, a domineering man with whom he had crossed swords when he had worked for him before.

He had desperately wanted the job, needing it for the select little gang finishing off at the catholic church, so he had ensured acceptance of the estimate by swallowing his principles and pricing on the bottom line.

When the phone rang he extended an arm automatically, still preoccupied with the Arbuthnot plan. The caller was an articulate woman with a posh accent, and he was surprised when she introduced herself as the fiancée of Harry of Aylesbury — they were, she said, to be married at the weekend — and requested information about his employment.

"I am sorry, miss," Thomson replied regretfully, "but that is not something I can divulge without Harry's permission."

"No, no, no! You don't understand," the voice at the other end of the line responded. "I wish only to know in what capacity he is employed."

Sensing potential trouble, Thomson replied carefully.

"As his fiancée, I should have thought you would know that. However, I will see Harry and urge him to make known to you the nature and details of his employment. You will appreciate I can hardly discuss a man's job with a third party, even if you are his fiancée."

She was not pleased.

The call had broken his concentration and when he replaced the phone he pushed his chair back, hoisted his feet on to the desk, loosened his tie, filled and lit his pipe, then proceeded to day-dream away what was left of the afternoon. In his anxiety over the work programme, he had forgotten it was Thursday, and the hymn singing of the Mothers' Union coming from the chapel just over the wall at the bottom of the yard, lulled him into a comforting sense of well-being.

It could have been the chapel voices that stimulated recollection of the Roman Catholic church miles from base where he'd had a small hand-picked gang employed for the last nine months re-roofing, re-flooring and carrying out general remedial work. The centre portion of the roof had fallen in after lightning started a fire, and the tiled floor of the church had been extensively damaged.

It had been necessary to scaffold the whole of the interior almost to roof level, and temporary flooring was laid right over the scaffolding so that the roof could be repaired with minimal damage and disturbance to the rather fine architectural features of the church.

In the beginning, when Thomson visited the site with the architect, he had been particularly requested to ensure that the dozen or so gaudily-painted stone statues ranged along the aisles on either side of the church be protected before the work was started.

"And," ordered the architect, an over-zealous soul, "you must see to it that your men remember at all times where they are, that no bad language is used, and *No Smoking*!"

"Right you are," Thomson promised, and at the first opportunity he passed on the instruction to Michael, his trusted foreman.

When the architect introduced him to the priest in charge, Thomson couldn't but wonder just how many Father O'Reillys had been spawned by the Hibernian branch of the Holy Roman Empire. Right away they were invited to his lodgings nearby for a refreshment, and he turned out to be a lovely, jovial Friar Tuck of a fellow, a man in his sixties, used to keeping the wheels of office well oiled, and one intent at all times on getting his own way.

Even before the end of the first week after the scaffolding was erected, the priest, peremptorily and without a by-your-leave, cancelled the architect's "no smoking" diktat.

"All day long," he explained to Thomson, "there was a continual procession up and down the ladders and out to the WC at the back for a puff. That's not only time consuming, but not in the men's best interests. Poor fellows, they're worn out by the afternoon."

A smile spread across Thomson's features as, brooding, he recalled a subsequent visit to the church when, on entering, he became instantly aware that two of the statues were missing. Alarmed, he sought out Michael who referred him to Father O'Reilly.

"It's like this, Mr Thomson," he explained, grinning broadly, "every time I stood in the pulpit, there they were: on my left St Patrick, on my right the pregnant Mary. Whenever I came into church, they were there searching my face for a glimmer of understanding, complaining about their coloured ugliness — imagine painting stone! — pleading for absolution.

"So I calls down St Michael, leader of the celestial

army, and I says to him, 'Michael', I says, 'this is what I wants you to do, me boy. . . .' "

His eyes twinkled, his mouth watered and, taking Thomson by the arm, he invited, "Come on into me hovel and we'll hiv a wee snifter."

The girl in the front office knew Thomson hated to be disturbed when he was enjoying the hymn singing on Thursday afternoons, so, as she knocked quietly on the door before entering his room, she quite expected a rebuke or, at the very least, a scowl.

Surprisingly, however, she found him to be in quite a good mood, abstraction having softened his habitual crustiness.

"Begging your pardon, Mr Thomson, but if you'd sign the letters I could get off to the post office. And. . ." she hesitated ". . . there's a lady downstairs waiting to see you."

"Oh? A *lady*, you say?" He took his feet off the desk. "Who is she and what's she want?"

"Name's Mrs Arbuthnot. I don't know what she wants."

Thomson didn't like dealing with ladies, a fact of which the girl was well aware. In any case, he reflected, the woman had no right to be poking her nose in. It was her architect who should be dealing with whatever was on her mind.

He took his time. Adjusting his collar and tie and humming to the strains of *Rock of Ages* wafting through the open window from the chapel, he signed his letters and re-knotted his shoe laces.

No doubt about it, Mrs Arbuthnot was top drawer. Everything about her said so. Even before she spoke, her whole aura indicated that she had generations of upper class blood in her veins which, no doubt, accounted for the lack of compunction in treading where her architect was paid to tread. In fact, as she rattled on,

Joined in the hymn singing with the Mother's Union

Thomson wondered why she employed an architect at all, for, patently, she was no amateur in the business of house building detail, handling her facts with lofty precision. Clearly, it wasn't the first time she'd had a house built.

He was still under the influence of his introspection, but, as he listened to Mrs Arbuthnot, he could feel all the good that had been done by Father O'Reilly and the faith restoring hymn singing matrons draining away.

He squared his shoulders and took out his tobacco pouch, a sure sign that he was preparing to regroup his thoughts.

"Do you mind, Mr Thomson? I have an allergy problem — tobacco smoke. I'm asthmatic."

Yes, thought Thomson, and that's not all you are. Obediently, however, he laid aside pipe and pouch.

On the face it, her visit had a two-fold purpose. First, she wanted his personal assurance that the contract period agreed upon would not in any circumstances be exceeded, and secondly, that all materials used would be of the best quality.

Reasonable enough, one might think, but Thomson was not so sure.

"But ma'am, you have ample cover on both points under the terms of the contract. No builder wants to force an architect to operate a penalty clause, and where the specification is not specific, provision has been made for certain material samples to be submitted for approval before use. Your architect is supposed to be your agent. We take instructions from him."

This was really a trifle more pointed than intended. She responded sharply, almost angrily.

"That does not preclude my having direct contact with you. After all, I'm paying the bill and am entitled to be satisfied in my own way. I have my reasons for being concerned about the completion date being strictly adhered to, and I'll thank you to remember that."

Thomson realised that the probable main object of her visit was to give him and his set-up the once-over. It had happened before many times, but never when an architect was involved.

She would keep rubbing him up the wrong way. Here she was, actually telling him off for pointing out that he looked to the architect for instruction. He was quite within his rights, of course, but her ladyship was getting under his skin, and he would have to be careful she didn't goad him into further indiscretion. There was nothing he resented more than a visitor without an appointment interrupting his Thursday hymn singing session.

But there was more to it than mere reaction to her visit, for early on in life he had taken a scunner to the la-de-da superior accents of some of the characters he had to do business with. The upper crust sound became anathema to him, and he had, over the years, grown more and more sensitive to its namby-pamby, dilettante effete resonance.

Some, like Mrs Arbuthnot, were genuine topdrawer — couldn't help it, born to it — didn't know any better. Some acquired it and like all fakes, were a bit pathetic.

And the men, especially the public school types, were worse than the women because they appeared emasculated, superficial, almost coquettish even when, in reality, they were nothing of the sort.

By the sound of her, Harry's fiancée was of the same kidney. He bristled at the thought of the telephone conversation. The cheek of the woman!

But this Mrs A. was the daddy of them all. The very precision of her voice sickened him. He was relieved when she took herself off and he hoped she wouldn't come back.

It had certainly not escaped Harry's notice that Alice, the landlady's daughter, had been offhand with him for the past two days, avoiding his company whenever possible and looking down her nose, so he was both surprised and pleased when she accepted his invitation to go out for a drink.

Ever since he came down to work in Pickstock, he had lodged with them in their little terraced home, striking up a close friendship, especially with the daughter, a girl of about twenty, receptionist to a local dentist; smart, pretty and very well-disposed towards him. From the beginning, they had got on remarkably well, so much so that both looked forward very much to having the house to themselves; especially on Wednesdays when the mother, widowed too young for comfort and anxious to circulate, was in the habit of spending the evening in a cinema-cum-bingo hall up the street.

Of course, with his easy conversational style he had flannelled Alice along, painting a rosy future of conjugal bliss and hinting generally at great times to come; such inducements, however, were quite superfluous because, despite a certain reluctance to declare her feelings, she had fallen for him hook, line and sinker. All she thought about, all she wanted was Harry, Harry, Harry.

It was early evening and there were not many people in the *Cherry Tree*.

They sat at a little table in the corner of the room, she with her gin and tonic, he with his pint of best bitter, a local brew much favoured in Pickstock pubs.

When he made to take her hand in his, she drew back sharply.

"Why do you *have* to go home at weekends?"

"I've always done it, ever since I came down here. You know that."

"Why?"

"It's my old girl, she expects it."

"Are you sure it's your *old* girl?"

His brows creased. "Who else? Why do you ask?"

She took a sip from her glass and looked him steadily in the eye.

"I ask because a little bird tells me you've gone and got yourself hitched."

Dumbfounded, panic-stricken, he grabbed at his tankard and gulped, only for the beer to go down the wrong way. For the moment she had quite scrambled his senses.

Slowly recovering, he forced a laugh and spluttered, "Would I be sitting here talking to you if I had?"

"You might."

"Oh, Alice, please stop messing about. You know I love you — I've told you often enough. I think you like me too, though you've never got round to admitting it. I'm daft about you . . . I idolise you!"

"I know I shouldn't," she replied, obviously affected, "but curiously, I believe you, and . . . you might as well know I feel the same way about you. But you've gone and mucked it up, haven't you? Oh, Harry, Harry, what have you done to us?"

Stifling a sob, she changed her tone, "If you haven't got married, prove it!"

Torn between the ecstasy of having wrung from her at last an admission of affection, and the agony of the predicament he found himself in, he gripped the table hard.

"How can I? When you're married you don't get a ring poked through your nose. What can I do?"

"You can tell the truth."

"I swear to tell the truth: I love you Alice. Give us a kiss and make up."

"You haven't answered my question yet," she reminded him. "Besides, I don't think your Isabel would take kindly to that."

Again, completely taken aback, he floundered on.

"What's she got to do with it? She's not written to you!? he cried, aghast.

"She's got quite a lot to do with it. She's the one you're supposed to have wed." Then, noticing his extreme discomfiture she said, "No, she hasn't written to me. As far as I'm aware, she doesn't even know I exist."

His face pictured his relief which, however, was short-lived as she continued, ". . . no-one else has written either . . . but there are other ways of passing information."

Alice slowly and carefully opened her handbag, rummaging inside almost as if seeking to prolong his agony. She then took something out, concealing it in her hand. Slowly, she returned the bag to the seat beside her, still keeping an eye on Harry.

"Oh, no, she hasn't written to *me*. But she's sent this to my mother. . . ."

Transfixed, he watched as, between finger and thumb, she held up a little white box, on the lid of which was embossed a bluebird with a ribbon in its beak bearing a message in silver lettering.

"It's a piece of cake — *your* wedding cake! Not inappropriate is it for a bride to send a piece of cake to the bridegroom's landlady?"

Without waiting for a reply, calmly, silently, she opened the box, took out the contents and removed the greaseproof wrapping. With great deliberation, she dropped the piece of cake into Harry's half empty pint pot, the beer slopping over on to the table.

"Now you've got your cake," she exploded, "and you can bloody well eat it — go on! — dry it out and warm it up for your supper!"

The tears were trickling down her cheeks as, rising, she banged a shin on the table leg. Picking up her glass she threw what was left of the gin and tonic in his face and, sobbing, stumbled out of the room.

Stunned, Harry wiped a hand across his cheek and after sitting immobile for several minutes, went over to the counter and downed a double Scotch. With a dozen pairs of eyes following his every move, he left the pub, face strained, shoulders hunched.

By the following morning every man on site was acquainted with the news of how Harry came by his come-uppance and, at the break, questions, comments and suggestions flew around the shed like confetti.

"'Arry! I could just eat a bit o' that cake."

"Always knew 'e were a dark 'orse."

"Anyway, 'e needn't expect a whip round for a weddin' present — we wasn't invited."

"Wasn't invited! 'Course we wasn't invited. 'Arry's in 'igh society. Who's gonna invite the 'oi poloi to a society wedding?"

"If I was you, Harry, I'd tie a knot in it."

"Try bromide — they say it works wonders."

"I met a posh dame once: for the life of me I couldn't make out what she were blatherin' about."

After the lull which followed, Tabby said wistfully "Shame 'bout Alice, though. Nice girl. Had a fancy for her myself."

Mick, busy re-plaiting his pigtail after drying his hair in front of the stove, paused and looked daggers at Harry. Unbeknown to anyone, he'd had an eye on Alice for quite some time and, although lacking proprietorial interest — he hardly knew the girl — was concerned about her treatment at the hands of a workmate. His catholic upbringing rose in his gorge, demanding something, he knew not what.

"You're a rotten sod, Harry. Why don't you bugger off back to Aylesbury? We got enough of your kind here."

"Don't be like that, Mickie," Harry persuaded placidly. "We've all got our bad habits, you know. If you didn't have a bad habit you'd head straight for the big time: depravity, corruption, villainy. A bad habit is your safety valve. Take me: a man of naturally weak character, I'm putty in the hands of any woman who takes a fancy to me. . . ."

"Ain't we all!" came a voice from the dim recesses.

". . . but a bad habit is not only a safety valve, it's a necessity, and I can state with absolute certainty that every man jack in this shed's got *his* bad habit, be it booze, dogs, women, horses or whatever."

Coke fumes and tobacco smoke mingled with the aroma of fried bacon and sausages. It was pay day and a fry-up had been arranged by tea boy Tommy, a war veteran whose poor old bloodshot eyes teardropped continually, giving the bucket brew — or, so claimed Stan — an elusive and distinctive flavour much appreciated by the discriminating.

The promise of a tasty snack and the excitement promoted by the news of Harry's love tangle combined to create an air of expectancy in the Nissen.

"Since you seem to have taken a sordid interest in my situation," continued Harry, "and are in possession of some of the facts, I might as well explain further — which, as you may be aware, is another of my bad habits. . . ."

There was nothing Harry liked better than to have the bit between his teeth; even a punctured heart had to play second fiddle to the necessity of soul display or harangue. Loquacity toned him up, conditioning and aerating the mind.

Like a group of youngsters waiting to be told a story, they all settled down round the stove, only to be disappointed when, for once, Harry was unnaturally brief, giving not even an abridged version of events at the

Cherry Tree, when what they expected was intimate detail.

"I married the wrong girl, didn't I? Couldn't wait. Got dazzled by the promise of a luxury flat and thirty pieces of silver to go with it."

There followed a lengthy pause.

"That's it, then? We're not to be told what happened at the *Cherry Tree*?" Thus did Stan speak up for the rest.

"You all know what happened at the *Cherry Tree*. There's no way I'm gonna enlarge on my bad habits."

"Well, I'll be blowed! Ain't yer gonna tell us 'bout them toffs you've got yourself mixed up with? Yer la-de-da missus and the rest of it?"

The Scots carpenter, who had been deep in thought, digesting Harry's bad habit dialectic, intervened somewhat irrelevantly.

"M' grannie, she had an awfa' bad habit: a porridge drawer."

This threw the listening group into mental disarray.

"Wot in hell's name you on about," asked Stan, while Twiggy's lower jaw dropped, lips parting in a comical expression of wonderment.

"Wot's a porridge drawer?"

"Well, you see, m'gran'faither worked in Carron Iron Works and was always first man on the job in the morning to see tae the furnaces. So the auld girl, fed up wi' rising at four in the morning, made enough porridge on Sundays to last the rest of the week."

"Blimey!"

"There wis yin o' yon auldfashioned chest o' drawers in the kitchen — nane o' y'r fancy units in them days — and she'd empty the porridge intae a drawer lined wi' American cloth. When it cooled it was a gey solid mass, and she'd tak' a kitchen knife and divide it intae six."

"Bloody hell! Always knowed you were a rough lot, but. . . ." Will ran out of words.

"Och aye, so we are, right enough. Anyway, there it was: each mornin' she'd tak' oot a hunk o' porridge, stick it in a pan on the range, and hey presto. . . . Believe you me, I wisnae awfa' fond o' that porridge, and naether wis gran' faither. He wis a mild-mannered man, never openly criticised onybody in his life, but he confided to me it wis an awfa' bad habit m' granny'd got intae."

As heavy rain began drumming on the corrugated tin roof, the men in their different ways thought about the porridge drawer and the breakfast scene in that Scottish kitchen long ago.

"Never mind 'bout yer bleed'n' porridge. Wot 'bout 'Arry's matrimonial problems? What's to be done about it?" demanded Stan.

There was no dearth of ideas.

"I think 'e could get a divorce on the grounds he made a mistake: married the wrong girl."

"Yeah! He could say he fell off the scaffold, got concussed, had blackouts and lost his memory — didn't know what he was doin' — bet 'e knowed wot 'e were doin' all right on the honeymoon — then he could marry Alice."

"Alice wouldn't have him now if he begged her to take his luxury flat *and* his pieces of silver," Mick sneered.

". . . he could plead he wisnae capable, no able t' dae his stuff, couldnae perform. . . ."

"Hey, wait a minute, wait a minute!" Harry protested. "I'm not exactly a bleed'n' eunuch, you know."

"Wot about the posh Isabel? Wot's she gonna say when she hears about Alice? You won't 'alf get wot for, 'Arry."

This triggered Tabby's reflective mood.

"Remember Willie gettin' wot for when we did the

war damage job in Wimpole Street? That dame, she 'ad a plum in 'er mouth too, but we'd never 'eard 'alf the swear words she shot at Willie! An' all 'e done was repaint the kitchen winder the wrong colour."

Outside, the rain was tipping cats and dogs and, when he stuck his nose round the door, Bill Sodder, the foreman, reluctantly agreed it was no good attempting to start work yet awhile.

Thomson barged in, soaked to the skin. He'd been meeting the council surveyor on site to agree an interim payment and, with the sudden and unexpected deterioration in the weather, sought sanctuary in the shed, which in any case he had been intending to visit later.

The day had started bright, though there had been a deal of inclement weather in the last few weeks and shed money had continued to erode the slim profit margin of the current fixed price contract.

Just as he liked to keep a kind of tentative contact with the Almighty during the Wesleyan Chapel hymn singing sessions, so, doffing his cloth cap, Thomson would periodically re-cement fellowship with the men on their own ground. He felt a compulsion to renew association, to restate fraternity, to relink with his working class background and so forestall complete severance of the umbilical cord. The truth, of course, was that for one reason or another he had never really been fully confirmed into middle class society despite business success and golf club membership, so had to be content with a foot in each camp.

He enjoyed having a mugga and a jaw with the chaps; he felt at home with them and was generally accepted into their deliberations because they sensed him to be mostly on their side of the fence.

When they let slip the subject of their present concern, Thomson said to Harry, "I told you you should've let your lady know about your job. By the sound of her she expected you to be, at the very least, a junior partner."

"Maybe guv, but she knows better now. Anyway, I'm glad I'm a carpenter; I never wanted to be anything else. It was my dad had the big ideas, the over-weaning ambition. But, I'm not complaining. If it did nothing else, education loosened me tongue."

"You could say that again," murmured Mick, still nursing his moral indignation.

"What's she like, 'Arry, this posh wife of yours?" Will asked, curious.

"Toffee-nosed, talks like Barbara Cartland," he replied. "But she's a lovely girl. My dad thinks the world of her." He fumbled in his jacket pocket. "Here's a picture of her in a bathing suit."

Handed round, the photo of the scantily clad Isobel produced exclamations of admiration laced with crude remarks.

The Scots carpenter gave it a perfunctory glance.

"Nae red flannel petticoats noo to stretch the imagination!" he sighed.

Thomson looked across at Harry and said, "You must have met Mrs Arbuthnot when you pitched that roof at Riverbank Close?"

"She wasn't around when I was there, guv."

"You don't know what you missed. You should hear her! Puts you in mind of a high class elocution teacher suffering from adenoidal rickets."

"Sounds very like my Isobel."

Harry stared thoughtfully at Thomson.

"Have you noticed" he said, "nobody seems to take it seriously. It's the one thing that epitomises, promotes and prolongs class division. 'Bout time it was broken."

"Wot you on about," Tabby enquired innocently.

"The sound barrier! the bloody sound barrier —

that's what I'm on about, you stupid bugger — those great, pompous twits that talk posh beyond the endurance of the likes of us." He made a gesture of despair, as if acknowledging that it would be quite impossible to make any significant inroads on Tabby's ignorance.

"Ah, but fair do's, fair do's," said Stan. "Them posh folk might think the same about us lot, that we're thick because we speak a different lingo — plain English."

Will recalled his wartime experience.

"In the army we had a company commander that talked posh. We was always laughin' at him, takin' him off, but just the same he were a plucky little sod."

"When you live with it," said Harry to Thomson again, "you either get used to it or you become more exasperated. I get more exasperated. We hadn't been wed a week 'fore I realised I'd have to get a divorce on the grounds of vocal incompatibility." Pensively, he added, "Shame, really, 'cos she's a great girl, and very fond of me."

Still smarting from the lash of Harry's tongue, Tabby growled, "You don't bloody deserve her, the way you carry on."

"I know, I know, isn't that just what I've been trying to tell you? I'm putty in the hands. . . ."

Mick, the only man in the shed with obvious religious convictions, had been waiting for a chance to quiz Thomson about the church job.

"You'll have met Father O'Reilly, Mr Thomson?"

"Oh yes, a fine man, a fine man."

"So he is. I've met him several times, he being a great friend of Father Hamlyn, the Pickstock priest, who you will know, of course?"

"Certainly, certainly. A man of great charm and much learning."

"I hear tell," continued Mick after a moment's hesitation, "there was a bit of a shindy 'bout some statues belonging to the church?"

"A shindy? There's been some very conflicting stories going the rounds — but a shindy? No, no. What happened was this: the roof was completed and the scaffolding cleared away, but when they started to lift the damaged tiling near the altar, the floor fell in.

"Apparently, in former times, there had been a crypt which had been partially filled in with rubble. A rotten floor joist gave way and *there* was a damn great hole! But — and this is the interesting bit — when Father Reilly is called to inspect it, he's quite calm, in fact beams all over his face, raises his eyes to heaven and is heard to murmur, 'Thank you, Lord, thank you'. Turning to Michael, he says, 'Michael, me boy, here's what I wants you to do. . .'

"And what d'ye think? He orders him to clear out all the rubble and make preparation for a burial!"

By this time all the men were listening eagerly, hanging on to his every word, so Thomson continues.

"So, the rubble is cleared out, and the priest tells Michael to have the crypt floor screeded, using quick setting. In due course, one by one — in the same order, mind you, and facing the same way as when standing up in the aisles — all the statues were lowered into the crypt, the last rites read and the flooring consolidated.

"'And,' says Father O'Reilly, with a gleam in his eye, 'no-one can complain that they didn't get a daecent burial: they're still in church, laid to rest in consecrated ground'!"

"Well I'll be damned!" Will reacted for them all.

"And there they lie," continued Harry as though he were on the stage at Stratford, "in the vault, all ship-shape and Bristol fashion, ready to mystify some future archaeologist who will analyse the whys and the where-fores of his remarkable find, no doubt speculating that they were totem images meaningful to a longsince vanished race and secreted away to avoid desecration at the hands of vandals in time of war."

"Amen," said Thomson, well pleased with the carpenter's summing-up.

"An' wot 'bout this Arbuthnot job, guv?" piped up Stan, concerned that Thomson was showing signs of leaving. "Found out yet who pinched the fireplace?"

Thomson scowled. It was a sore point with him at the moment. Apparently, Michael — the same Michael who had been in charge at the catholic church — had discovered one morning that a slabbed fire surround delivered and built into place the previous day, ready for the plasterer to make good, had overnight been neatly hacked out from the living room chimney breast and carted off, no-one knew exactly how or by whom.

And it wasn't as if it was a particularly valuable fireplace, far from it.

Knowing his client, Thomson had expected to be fussed and goaded to produce some fantoosh surround difficult to make and emblazoned with figured tiles nigh impossible to obtain. Not a bit of it!

In the event, Mrs Arbuthnot had insisted on seeing the supplier herself — a builder's merchant specialising in bespoke and off-the-peg fire surrounds — picked a standard design with in-stock tiles and was so accommodating that the department manager complimented her on her choice and dubbed her "a real toff".

Of course, being a standard design it was dead easy to repeat, and a replacement, ordered and delivered with all speed, had only yesterday been set in place, securely fixed and the plastering made good.

In response to Stan's question, Thomson, not now in the mood for further palaver, simply replied "No", at the same time drawing Bill Sodder's attention to the fact that the rain had now abated. He hurried out of the shed.

No sooner had he stepped inside his office and removed his wet clothes, than the phone rang. It was Michael.

"I've been trying to get you all morning, Mr Thomson." He paused. "You're not going to believe this, guv!"

"Oh? Why's that?"

"That fireplace: it's been lifted again — vamoosed, gone, disappeared without trace — taken out clean as a whistle!"

For a full minute there was a deathly silence.

"What in hell's name's going on?"

The mystery was never solved. The culprit, whoever he was, had well covered his tracks, leaving not a crumb of incriminating evidence; a building trade worker without a doubt.

It became a favourite topic of speculation in the sheds, to the men a riddle every bit as intriguing as the Marie Celeste or the Princes in the Tower.

And Alice?

Well, Harry did get a divorce, but alas! by then the magic had gone, the fine, wondrous once-in-a-lifetime idolatry had taken itself off. She married her dentist boss's son and to all appearances lived happily ever after, though if Harry was anything to go by, with the spectre of true love raising its head from time to time, gnawing away at the might-have-been.

Hods on Bet

THE boss had come on site during the temporary absence of the brickies who, grumbling, had been called away to attend to a nuisance job Whealer had been putting off for months.

Left behind on his own to load the second lift, the hod carrier was hard at it when he heard the car draw up.

"Hey there, Chris!" Whealer called out. "Come on down and have this can of beer."

Chris squinted, muttering to himself, "Hullo! wonder what he wants now?"

However, he greeted the boss amicably enough, joining him on the makeshift bench outside the shed. It was a humid day, so the beer was acceptable and timely.

Almost right away they started a discourse on thirst.

"It's all right for you," argued Chris. "You can have a drink any time you like — between sites, just stop your car and hop into the nearest pub."

"But I don't wish to drink at any old time in any old pub," Whealer countered. "I don't do enough hard physical work to want a drink like you want a drink. I envy you your thirst. Have you ever thought how much sweeter that beer is to you than to me? You've earned it by the sweat of your brow."

"Ah, but just the same, it must be great to stop and have one whenever you want," persisted the hod carrier, wistfully.

"It's always what we haven't got or what we can't have that we want," Whealer laughed. "Have you noticed that, Chris? The difference between man and the lower orders."

As they finished their drink the guv'nor turned to him

and said, "Chris, I'd like you to do me a favour."

The hod carrier stiffened. It wasn't the first time he'd been asked to do Whealer a favour and, from experience, he knew such favours to be inconvenient, time consuming and unprofitable. He might have guessed there would be a price to be paid for the beer!

As it turned out, for once he was wrong, and the upshot was as providential as it was unexpected.

For many years, Whealer had been friendly with Tickey Friday, the Mayor of Pickstock — his father had been the town's watch repairer and knick-knack man — Tickey being the well-to-do director of a builders' merchant conglomerate operating widely throughout the area. Whealer was godfather to his daughter, Sarah, now a ravishing eighteen-year-old blonde who had attracted the attentions of many of the young fellows in the locality; so much so that it had become something of a worry to her parents.

"I tell you what I want you to do, Chris. When you knock-off I'd like you to load the dumper with three barrows of three-quarter ballast, one of soft sand and half a dozen bags of cement, and deliver to Friday's in Chalk Lane, the Laurels. Mrs Friday will tell you where to dump it." He paused, then, "You can stick an extra half hour on your time sheet," he concluded magnanimously.

When, later, Chris arrived at the house a few hundred yards uphill from the site, he found Mrs Friday to be out. At his ring, the door was opened by the stunning Sarah who was having great difficulty in restraining a huge, shaggy dog which she was holding by the collar. The dog, barking wildly, seemed intent on making contact with Chris.

"You can let your dog go, he won't bother me," Chris told her calmly.

She took him at his word and was not a bit surprised

to see the animal lunge forward. However, tail wagging furiously, it planted its paws squarely on Chris's shoulders and proceeded to lick his face. Evidently, it was delighted to see him.

"You're highly honoured," Sarah said, amazed at the dog's behaviour. "He doesn't usually go to strangers — he goes for them. You certainly have a way with dogs!"

"It's my charisma," Chris replied off-handedly. Then, abruptly, "Anyway, where do I shoot this stuff?" pointing to the dumper.

It wasn't that he was totally unconscious of her looks or her charm, but he was damned if he was going to let her see the effect her nearness had on him. Stuck up bitch! He'd seen her kind before, contact usually resulting in the meteing out of the classical cold shoulder treatment. He had no intention of giving her that kind of satisfaction.

"I think it would be all right if you put it over there," she answered demurely, pointing.

He was just finishing off-loading when she called from the front door, "If you'd like to go round to the kitchen door, I'll pour you a cold drink."

Chris bristled. Just what he would have expected. The tradesman's entrance for him!

"No thank you," he replied evenly. "I'm in a hurry."

And that was that. At least, he thought it was, until the following day when Whealer came on site.

"Had Mr Friday on the phone this morning. You shot that load of sand and ballast in the wrong place. All right! All right! I know it wasn't your fault, but could you go round sometime today and shift it to the rear of the garage. And, by the way, the brickies won't be back till late afternoon, so meanwhile perhaps you could dab some pink primer on them door and window frames you've had from the yard."

The most significant sign of old age is when tiredness is no longer a nuisance, but a pleasure.

Sarah's ageing grandad — the watch repairer emeritus — subscribed to this view and, although energetic physical movements were now limited to short toddles twice a day, his mental activities, seemingly moribund to those around him, were in fact unimpaired. Like so many elders, he was very good at fostering the impression of being maudlin and muddle-headed.

A widower, he now occupied a granny flat tacked on to the Laurels at his son's insistence, and such leisure hours that remained after mending the odd watch or clock for friend or relation were spent in his recliner chair on the little terrace overlooking the grounds at the back of the house, or perhaps dozing with a book or scanning the death notices in his favourite quality paper — with a satisfaction always keen, sometimes grim, occasionally mournfully; a practice not vouchsafed to younger mortals.

When the urge came, he would take a stroll round the garden and exchange a few thoughts with Charlie, gardener and odd job man, his intimate of many years standing who had been in his employ before coming to the Laurels. In fact, his one condition in agreeing to removal to the flat from his own home, had been that Charlie came with him, to be taken on the staff and to continue to enjoy the same conditions of employment; which fitted in very well, for Tickey, having hitherto put up with the part-time services of an unenthusiastic learner-gardener, welcomed the prospect of professional skill and muscle.

Charlie's conditions of employment had been promulgated many years before when the elder Friday, incensed by the expropriatory habits of a previous employee, had put an ad in the situations vacant column of the local paper, an ad widely remarked upon:

> Gardener/general factotem: good all-rounder wanted to take charge of one acre, including vegetable plot and small orchard. No gratuities or bonus, no produce or firewood, no perks of any kind. In lieu, a payment of two pounds a week will be made above the going rate for the job. Apply. . . .

As a continual reminder, the £2 payment was always handed over in a separate envelope on wages day, although over the years the growing friendship between master and man gradually relaxed the constraint of the initial decree.

One morning, after breakfast, while Charlie was busy weeding the vegetable patch, old man Friday carefully picked his way along the narrow grass path between the cabbages and peas.

"Who's that young fellow-me-lad I see you talking to the last couple of nights, Charlie?"

"Oh, that's Chris, carries the hod for Whealer — good lad. Keeps wicket for Pickstock and they say he could be in the county team if he had a mind to it. Good worker, too."

"What's he doin' round here?"

"Tickey said he could help me put in the foundations and lay a bit of brickwork for the new greenhouse at the back of the garage — in his spare time, of course. It's all above board, been arranged."

"Oh! Only, I see him talking to Sarah. Are they thick?"

"Not that I know of."

"If he's not careful he'll kill himself on that damn great motorbike he runs about on; nasty, noisy, treacherous things; always did think so even in my own Norton days. With the traffic hereabouts it's no wonder they cost over three hundred to insure. Did you know that, Charlie?"

"No. But he's a steady lad is Chris. Come to think of it, I wouldn't be at all surprised if there *is* something in the wind between him and Sarah."

When Chris had returned to shift the sand and ballast to the back of the garage, Sarah had been waiting for him.

"There was no occasion for you to be so brusque yesterday. I suppose it would have been all right if I had asked you into the lounge? Is that what was biting you?"

Chris, taken aback by this frontal attack, could only stammer, "Sorry about that, but I *was* in a hurry."

Unconvinced, she flounced off back to the house, at the same time calling over her shoulder, "And if you should want a drink before you go, it'll have to be the kitchen, like it or not that's where we keep our fridge."

All the time he was to-ing and fro-ing with the sand and ballast he was thinking furiously about what she had said. She was right, of course, but there was just the slightest hint of something else. Could it be interest, he speculated.

The previous day she must have detected the drift in his thinking by the tone of his voice. Now, he was in a fix. He knew that if ever he was going to make contact with her again it would have to be in the kitchen. She certainly was a dazzler. Already, she had laid the spell on him. And she knew just how to throw down the gauntlet.

He'd have to give in, of course, couldn't help himself. When, at his knock, she came to the kitchen door, he grinned like the village loon, touched the peak of his forage cap in rustic fashion and, broadly vernacular, whined, "Beg pardon, miss, d'ye think I could have a drop of water from the kitchen tap?"

"Come on in, you great Charley," she answered readily, obviously pleased and giving him a little push. Both laughed out loud.

That was it. They'd changed gear. They got on like a house on fire, and when, a week later, he asked her to be his guest at the cricket club dinner dance, she accepted with unfeigned delight, despite the fact that her father in his official capacities as Mayor and vice-president of the club, would almost certainly be there as well.

He was! and he didn't particularly like what he saw, but, give him his due, for the moment put a good face on it, consoling himself with the thought that after all Chris *was* a damn good all-rounder.

When Tickey got home after the do, it was only natural he should debate with his wife the possibility of a permanent link-up between the hod carrier and their Sarah, for it was very evident she had been clean bowled. They did not like the look of things at all, though for different reasons.

She was worried that such coupling, with or without marriage lines, might have a devastating effect on her relationship with the top set, fearing that shock waves would engulf everyone within her circle. Becoming Mayoress had given a great fillip both to her ego and to her social standing.

Because she had always had money to burn, she ridiculed her husband's immediate preoccupation which was how much the hod carrier would expect by way of dowry, for he had no doubt at all that Chris thought he was on to a good investment, and had in prospect both fiscal and vocational advancement.

Tickey had had a bad week. His Volvo had contracted sticky valves, twice he'd missed the 7.20am to Paddington, and he fell out with his wife because she had massively overspent on the housekeeping for the second month running. Not only that, since his elevation to the mayoralty, additions to her wardrobe had been legion and bills had been coming in thick and fast.

She, too, had been under the weather. An enthusiastic

cook, in the last few days she had mucked up a special recipe for the WI bring and buy sale, and when, because of an oven-fault, she overcooked the weekend joint (a thing she had never done before in her life), and attempted to substitute a salad, she found she had run out of mayonnaise and that her one bottle of vinegar had well and truly mothered. It was all very tiresome and frustrating.

These considerations apart, misgivings about their daughter's future were understandable because they revived memories of their other offspring, John, who had married beneath him at nineteen, repented at twenty, and had been divorced at twenty-one. Not only that, but the day the decree nisi came through, he chucked his job, wheedled £500 from grandad, worked his passage to Australia, disappeared into the outback, since when his only contact with home was a picture postcard to Sarah from Alice Springs with, in the circumstances, the maddeningly humdrum and unrevealing message: "Having a lovely time — wish you were here — will write soon". And that was just eighteen months before Chris came on the scene.

So, who could blame the Fridays for the thought that it must be something in the blood? Perhaps a genetic hiccup.

However, Tickey played it cool on the grounds that it was all circumstantial supposition; but this proved to be shortlived, and his first interview with Sarah did nothing to allay his anxiety. Really, it made matters worse because it confirmed her resolve to get married as soon as possible. She could hardly wait — in contrast to Chris who, when the subject was mooted, back-tracked on his own desires and uncharacteristically, counselled caution and delay, which, naturally enough, made Tickey even more suspicious of the hod carrier's intentions.

One night in the *Nag's Head*, while having a quiet drink together, Chris told Sarah that he needed a bit more time to get together the wherewithal for the honeymoon and to complete negotiations for the two-up and two-down terrace cottage he was aiming to buy. Sarah was enthusiastic about the "dinky little cottage", but unfortunately impatience got the better of her.

"I don't really see why you object to my dad finding the money; at least let him pay for the repairs. It is a bit dilapidated."

"I know bloody well it's dilapidated," Chris snorted. "Isn't that why I'm getting two of my mates to give me a hand to knock it into shape?"

"I wish you wouldn't swear! I'm only trying to help."

He put an arm around her and gave her a little surreptitious kiss.

"I know! I know! I'm sorry about that. But I'm not sorry about anything else.

"Look, Sarah! I know exactly what your old man thinks. He thinks that I think I'm on to a good thing. I am, but not in the way he looks at it. I'm tickled pink to marry his daughter, but strange though it may seem, I don't want anything else. I've already told him that, but he doesn't believe me, so maybe you should try to put him right. And another thing, there's no need for him to buy us an expensive wedding present; a bed, a table and a few chairs and I'll be delighted. I don't intend to be in your father's pocket for the rest of my life. If you want to marry me — and I *know* you do — then you'll have to put up with my pay and conditions."

She held her hands aloft.

"Don't be so cross, darling! I accept! I accept your conditions . . . but maybe at Christmas and birthdays we could go round to the Laurels and live it up! Eh?"

He laughed at her persuasive, theatrical, bright-eyed eagerness.

"Oh, I won't be above sticking my snout in the trough occasionally. But when we marry you'll have to settle for being a hod carrier's wife instead of a managing director's daughter. If I didn't really think you were with me in this, I wouldn't marry you. . . ."

Pausing, he kissed her cheek. ". . . we'd just have to live in sin."

"You needn't bother about me Chris," she replied seriously. "I'm no gadfly. All I want is to marry you, have three kids and live happily ever after. I'll take my chance with you on keeping up with the Joneses."

Grandad came into the pub with Charlie. It was a weekly routine to exchange a couple of drinks on a Friday night. After acknowledging the young couple, they were about to settle at the bar when Chris called them over.

Right away, grandad turned to him and, quite seriously, said, "Last night I prayed to God you'd sell that blasted bike of yours."

"You what? You're having me on?"

Charlie, sensing tension, generalised, "I often pray — not for gimme gimme, but for understanding."

Side-tracked, grandad looked at him.

"There's really only one thing to pray for — if you haven't got it — and that's blind faith. I haven't got it, so I'm always praying for it. It would make everything so much more bearable; like marrying off one's favourite granddaughter to a motorbike fiend."

Chris was looking at them open mouthed.

"I *was* going to buy you a drink!"

"Well," Sarah commented, "what a subject! I thought you'd be asking how our plans were progressing?"

Chris was still thinking about grandad's opening gambit.

"As it happens, you needn't worry about the bike;

I'm selling it. Got to raise the wind somehow."

"Your grandad's sorted out a lovely present," Charlie said to Sarah. "You'll like it. In a way, it's quite practical; depends on how you look at it."

The penny did eventually drop with Tickey. At first it was a great relief. Then, new and unsuspected anxieties seeped in and both he and his wife went off on another tack. What would people think about Sarah living in a little scruffy old terraced cottage? It was all very well for folk to claim that everyone was more broadminded these days, that *now* they took no notice of circumstances like this; not like they used to. He didn't believe it. Experience told him things had altered very little in that direction. He could hear his fellow councillors sniggering behind his back.

When he reached for his cheque book, he was fiercely, firmly and finally rebuffed by the independent Chris.

Yet, Sarah's father was nothing if not reliant. He knew when to change tack and make the best of things.

Despite everything, he really began to respect the hod carrier, even to like him a bit, and Chris was astonished when, after a drink at the house one night, Tickey insisted that every single one of his mates on the building site be invited to the wedding reception to be held in a hired marquee in the grounds at the back of the Laurels.

"And this time it's no good arguing about who's going to pay. The bride's father always pays for the reception."

"I wasn't thinking about that, in fact it never entered my head. I was wondering if you realised what a rough house you could have on your hands?"

"On *my* hands?" Tickey looked at him slyly.

"I'm no bloody foreman!" Chris exploded, "no chucker-out!"

"How do you know?"

Chris gaped.

Very good at sowing seeds was Tickey, and a dab hand at delegating responsibility.

In the event, the wedding went off very well, as did the breakfast; making allowance for the natural playfulness of the men and their eagerness to take full advantage of the free booze.

Also, considering they were poles apart, Chris's parents got on remarkably well with their opposite numbers.

What made the day for the Fridays was the reappearance out of the blue of their son and heir; at least, it would have made their day had he not chosen to bring along a dainty Chinese girl with an Australian accent and an Oriental taste in black and gold pantaloons. Anyone could see they were devoted to one another, but consternation was hardly the word when she was introduced by John as his new wife.

It turned out that, arriving back in England three weeks earlier, he had funked reunion with his folks until, seeing an announcement of Sarah's wedding in the paper, he determined to attend the ceremony.

"What do you think of Ming Foo," he enquired tentatively of his father when they had a minute alone.

"Oh, very nice, very pretty, very decorative." Then, throwing discretion to the winds and trembling with suppressed indignation he spat out, "What I can't understand is why you had to *marry* her?"

"Expecting," replied the son, laconically.

Tickey had no answer to that.

The only real difficulty at the reception arose when Joey — he worked in the same gang as Chris — intent on "fair do's" after the toast to the bride and groom, and anxious that the virtues of his mate should not be overlooked in the all-round complimentary references to the bride — insisted on harangueing at length on the manliness and modesty of the bridegroom, extolling his ability as a worker and constancy as a friend. All of which would have been acceptable enough had the sentiments expressed been delivered succinctly and with comprehensive articulation. Unfortunately, Joey's cups had been overflowing for some time and only his mates, used to such meanderings, knew what he was on about. Determined to see that the bride did not get a monopoly of the limelight, and much to Chris's embarrassment, he would keep rabbiting on about what a good worker he was.

As a rule, a man who applied himself to his work diligently looked down his nose at any of his fellows who preferred inactivity.

"Joey? 'E's a lazy bugger," they would say on site. "'E's last 'ere in the morning, off like a shot 'fore knocking-off time, and missin' in between."

Chris's energy must have come from the distaff side of the family for his father reckoned to exert himself only on the bowling green. Thirty years' experience dodging the column at the local brewery had cemented a fine appreciation of the leisured life; *his* father, when introduced to his future daughter-in-law had bluntly warned, "I hope you realise you are marrying a gentleman without an estate".

But Chris, satisfied with his own workrate, tolerantly took the in-between view and was quite happy with Joey's ingrained indolence, fully accepting that there was plenty of room for all sorts; in fact had a sneaking admiration for the man because, not being one of those who lauded hard work for its own sake, concluded that if you were of that kidney you couldn't help it.

Conversely, as if proof were needed that nature moves in a mysterious way, Joey's approval, even when sober, of Chris's application to the job was almost lyrical, certainly adulatory. Right enough, there are many mansions.

When the chaps struck up, "For he's a jolly good fellow", Joey, satisfied that Chris had got his deserts, slid off his chair as though on rollers and collapsed in a crumpled heap on the floor, flies wide open, jacket and trousers whisky-slopped, out for the count.

To her mother's obvious displeasure, Sarah burst into an uncontrollable fit of giggling at the tableau effect of Joey's mates bending over his supine figure, exhibiting comical indecision as to how to cope with the unexpected contingency. She laughed so much that some of the guests were infected. Reaching out for support, she unfortunately overdid it and sent plates and glasses flying in all directions, with disastrous results to the sartorial elegance of some of her neighbours (including Whealer himself) who, however, aided no doubt by the liberality of the drink, took it all in good part.

Meanwhile, becoming aware that Tickey was eyeing him across the table, Chris, galvanised into action, strode across the room and took charge, with a muscular heave yanking Joey to his feet and, at the same time, inviting the men to remove him and themselves from the beano to the bar of the *Nag's Head*, where it had been arranged they would conclude their part in the celebrations.

As they left the marquee with loud expressions of appreciation and good luck, Chris bringing up the rear, Tickey's features relaxed into a complacent smirk; the boy, thought he, was coming along nicely, showing distinct promise. He'd do, might even in the fullness of time become a valued addition to the family stock, unlike that sinophile son of his who had been a pain in the neck ever since he left school, and was set fair to continue in the same prescription.

Even the hired tourer with the old-fashioned hood was part and parcel of grandad's wedding present. The newly-weds were over the moon when told that the old fellow — all his life a stickler for the pragmatic concept — had decided to be entirely unpractical in his choice, providing a fortnight's hotel accommodation in Jersey, plane tickets, hired car at the airport and wallet containing spending money; an ephemeral gift maybe, but one to be remembered long after the fish knives and forks, electric blankets and other traditionally favoured presents had gone to their last resting place. As far as the young couple were concerned, he couldn't have chosen anything better, though Sarah did have some difficulty in persuading her man to take the cash.

When Tickey remonstrated with his father for throwing his money about, the response was immediate.

"It's mine, ain't it? Anyway, Chris is the best thing that's happened to this family for a long time; fresh blood, self-reliance. I'll lay odds he'll turn up trumps!"

The canine incident came near the end of the honeymoon.

They had just left a shopping precinct when, without warning, a big, woolly airedale, on the prowl and sniffing keenly up and down the service road, dashed in front of them, leapt on to the back seat of their car and, sitting bolt upright, looked straight ahead through the windscreen.

Nonplussed, they stood on the pavement agape. Sarah was the first to recover and turning to Chris encouraged, "Well, go on then! You're the one with the charisma, remember?"

Reaching out hesitantly for the door handle, he was immediately repelled by the savage mein of the animal which, baring its teeth, snarled a warning that it would brook no interference.

"Good dog, good dog," Chris intoned softly, persuasively, trying another tack, but the airedale wasn't having any, and said so. It was not to be dislodged and, as if to underline this determination, sank its teeth into the sleeve of Chris's new sports jacket when, again changing tactics, he reconnoitred the rear.

"Whatever are we going to do," Sarah wailed, anxiously looking from the torn sleeve to the little group of shoppers that had congregated to watch the proceedings. It was only too obvious they thought it an hilarious situation.

Nobody knew whose dog it was or where it had come from. The people serving in the nearby chippy were too busy to offer any advice, and enquiries around elicited nothing at all helpful.

"I'd phone the police if I were you," recommended a big, burly blear-eyed man who said he'd once been bitten by an airedale, and gave it as his opinion that it would take a team of dog handlers to shift this one.

It seemed a good idea.

When the police arrived, a baton-wielding constable drove the dog off the back seat, though only after some difficulty, for it spurned preliminary blandishments and at first seemed set to retain possession. Unfortunately, the policeman had left his patrol car door open, a circumstance of which the dog took immediate advantage.

One bystander, a studious looking young man wearing a pair of enormous spectacles, judged the dog to be suffering from a car fixation — auto-fetish, he called it — and declared it to be in need of psychiatric treatment.

Already late for dinner at their hotel, Chris and Sarah thankfully departed the scene, leaving the constable still thwarted in his efforts to eject the airedale from the police car. Of course, he was now getting lots of encouragement and suggestions from the crowd which had swollen to demo proportions, most of the onlookers highly appreciative of the unexpected diversion.

"I thought dogs were attracted to you?" Sarah reflected on the way back to the hotel.

Chris grinned sheepishly.

"That first time at your house . . . that was because I already knew your dog. He used to come down to the site on the scrounge. I fed him scraps."

"So that was it! And here was I under the impression that you were one of those special people in tune with animals — like Mrs Woodhouse, blowing up horses' nostrils to prove she was friendly. Well, well! What a let down. Had I known, I might never have agreed to marry you," she teased. She leant on his shoulder and tousled his hair. "So, you're not so special after all, are you?"

Jake's Progress

"WE'LL have a wee blitzie before we go upstairs," announced Mrs Lappitt, poking the dying embers of the applewood fire and throwing on a dry, gnarled old log set aside for just such a purpose.

Sam, dozing comfortably in his Windsor chair, whisky glass on the mantelpiece within arm's reach, was startled by the sudden flare-up, in his agitation stubbing a toe against the fender and completely losing the thread of a very satisfying pipe-dream in which he had been getting the better of an awkward customer in an argument about extras.

"Wot you want to go an' do that for!" he admonished. "You know very well we can't go to bed leavin' a blaze like that."

Mrs L. gave him a sharp look but continued with her darning, from time to time pausing to dive a hand into a paper bag lying on the little carved table by the fireplace. She was a woman who, all her married life, had a penchant for Harris tweed and ginger chocolates, and whenever Sam wanted to get into her good books he would buy her some chocolates; in a box if he was especially anxious, or loose in a paper bag if he judged the emergency to be of a more transient nature.

The Harris tweeds she bought herself. It was almost a fetish and whenever she contemplated such an addition to her wardrobe, Sam would show his displeasure in the only way he dared; by taking the huff and acting dumb for a few days. Himself, he was partial to the fluffy chocolate box image of the ideal female, preferably flounced in silk, satin or lace, a fact of which his wife was totally unaware, though, even if she had been, she would only have berated him for a prig and a fool.

He realised instinctively that she'd had something in mind when she put that log on the fire, though he knew she was too fond of her bed to let a wee blitzie keep her from it for long.

Allowing him to simmer down a bit, she soon estimated that the time was ripe to broach the subject she had in mind.

"I saw Helen today. She's not been very well, you know."

Alerted, Sam responded cautiously, laconically, trying hard to keep the question mark out of his inflection.

"Uh-huh!"

"It's peptic ulcers and, as if that wasn't enough, she's got a hiatus hernia as well. She's been under the doctor, but there's little improvement."

Helen was Mrs L.'s niece who lived with her surveyor husband on the other side of Pickstock in one of those pretentious Victorian houses commonly described as Queen Anne front and Mary-Ann back. It occupied a corner site fronting a nice road, and more than once there had been overtures from developers interested in acquiring part of the more than ample back garden.

Sam reckoned that, at least in part, Helen kept in touch because it was handy having a relative whose husband was in the building trade; in her book a guarantee of quick service and cut price when the occasion arose. And, in fairness to Sam's thinking, those occasions had been only too frequent over the years, maintenance on such a property being reminiscent of painting the Forth Bridge.

"She was wondering if you could do a little job for them?"

"Oh ah!"

"They've got the damp coming through again in that

flat roof extension."

"Hard luck! Why can't Herbert do something about it? Got plenty of contacts with builders — or so he was telling me the last time I saw him. He's a surveyor, ain't 'e? Anyway, these days it's a specialist job. Nothing to stop him contacting a roofing firm same as I'd have to do."

"Oh Sam! surely it wouldn't hurt to do them a small favour. She's very down at the moment, what with being off colour and having his mother living with them. Poor thing! she doesn't know which way to turn."

"But Geraldine. . . .!" he protested — she would brook no diminutive — ". . . I'm stuffed up to the eye-balls. *I* don't know which way to turn either."

"Surely, Sam, you could spare half an hour to at least go and have a look at it?"

He knew perfectly well she would twist his arm un-mercifully until she got what she wanted, and having just bought his way out of the doghouse, did not relish a further period of internment.

"I'll see what I can do," he replied resignedly.

Actually, the last month had been a good one for the Lappitt organisation. He had solved one or two tricky problems; obtained, against fierce competition, a contract to build half a dozen council bungalows; completed the purchase of a small parcel of land with outline planning for three units — it had seen better days as an orchard, and he lost no time in grubbing-up several ancient apple trees to be split into logs and stacked in the yard near the back door of the office — and had managed to settle a long-standing argument on the final account of a house built for a local trades-man two years before.

So, the morning after the confab about Helen's flat roof, hands in pockets he strolled up and down the general office taking note of what was afoot, feeling pleased with himself and harbouring a benevolent outlook towards his fellow men.

Walking behind the typist's chair — she was fairly new to the job — he stopped suddenly, eyes popping.

"Jeannie! for god's sake girl! mind the platten, mind the platten!"

Startled, the girl looked up and, anxious to please, had the presence of mind to reply, "I will, Mr Lappitt, certainly I will," though she had not the remotest idea what he was talking about.

"Well, you're not doing it now, are you? That was the first thing I learnt when I started typing: always have a backing of at least two sheets to protect the platten. That way it'll last for years."

"Yes, Mr Lappitt."

Of course, he was merely asserting his authority. At best a two-finger man, he'd not touched a typewriter these twenty years or more.

After rifling through the post looking for cheques, he had barely settled down to work out the lorry journeys — a job he normally did the night before — when the telephone rang in the general office and Jeannie came on the tannoy.

"It's Fred on the phone, Mr Lappitt. There's been an accident. Jake's been taken to the cottage hospital."

It was generally recognised that Jake had always been, well, a little bit odd, odd but harmless. Sometimes he would be found playing with the children in the rec.; often he would be seen kicking and dribbling a tin can down the street; quite unselfconsciously, mind you. On the other hand, as far as his job was concerned, he was all there; in full possession of his marbles, as the saying goes.

Lately, however, Jake had been disturbed, not quite the man he had been. In a sudden spasm of help-thy-

Often seen dribbling a tin can down the street

neighbour fervour, he had taken a small bag of floor brads and a handful of sprigs from the yard stores and, as luck would have it, Lappitt, lately alerted about the shrinkage of sundry hardware items, caught him in the act.

It wasn't as if he stole for himself. He was doing it for his friend, Ben, amateur handiman and general dogsbody in the town's wet fish shop who, out of the kindness of his heart, had volunteered to do a few odd jobs for a poor old woman who lived in a rickety rented cottage nearby. Recently, she had lost her husband with cancer.

Lappitt read the riot act as you would expect, but let him off with a caution; he was much too good a hod carrier and labourer to be fired.

It preyed on Jake's mind. He took it badly and a kind of sickness got hold of him — not because he had been caught red-handed; oh no! The reason was that he couldn't convince his mates on site of the selfless motivation behind his action.

Even Mavis, his wife, who quite understood his feelings, could do nothing with him. Instead of going to the pub to play shove-ha'penny or crib and have his pint of old and mild, he took to roaming the countryside at weekends usually with his pair of war surplus binoculars for company (he'd always been interested in bird watching), but that only stirred up more trouble because, after being spotted a few times with glasses at the ready, it got about that he was a Peeping Tom.

In truth, it has to be said that he was not above refocusing when the occasion presented itself for, being Jake, he did not harbour the same inhibitions as other men. But that was quite fortuitous. There was not an ounce of premeditated peep in the man.

He became so restless in the night that his wife moved into the spare bedroom.

Drawing the bedclothes over his head, he would dream about his meanderings, but, mostly in a half awake stupor, would think about a particular lonely twisty lane lying out there in the darkness waiting for the dawn to bring along some social misfit, someone like him, for only such as he could share seclusion companionably with a twisty lane, watching the wildlife in the hedgerows or the tadpoles and amoebas in the ditches.

He knew he would have it all to himself and that he would be more than welcome because, since the coming of television, the local children didn't go near the place, preferring to sit on their rumps at home gaping at Star Wars or horrific movies or whatever mind boggling fodder happened to be on the menu.

Dream suffused into hallucination when, one night, the council surveyor recommended certain improvements incorporating a road widening scheme: and a group of quaint people — led by an ancient solicitor, a thirties hiker-biker — hit upon the idea of forming a Twisty Lane Preservation Society, and hopped in and out of the bedroom resolved to organise a demo against the surveyor's proposals.

Jake and the twisty lane merged, becoming one and the same.

He woke up startled when Mavis, alarmed at the noise he'd been making, shook him roughly and bellowed in his ear, "For god's sake, Jake, what's gotten into you?"

During the day he thought a lot about those people and their demo, but on balance came out against them for he decided they were simply infatuated with the idea of a twisty lane society and would only transform the lane into a kind of museum piece. They wouldn't give up their stinking motor cars, noisy mopeds, or anything else for that matter to lend a pen'orth of credence to their fancy talk.

Weak in the head he might be, but there were times

when his judgement was ahead of orthodox thinking.

Jake's fall from the scaffold followed another night of near delirium, the twisty lane syndrome persisting. He was clearly not fit for work, and if only he had heeded Mavis, who told him to go and see the doctor, it might never have happened. But he had a stubborn streak in him which surfaced especially when he was out of sorts.

The small gang of which he was a member, had been working on four singles in a cul-de-sac, a nice little development from which Lappitt expected great things. Each plot had been sold off separately with a contract to build, saving the purchasers a fair bit in solicitors' charges and stamp duty; and, with an eye to perks, the chaps had hoisted aloft on one of the houses a dog-eared standard left over from some past coronation celebration, a reminder to the customer that appropriate contribution in coin or liquid provender would not be amiss now that the structure was topped out. (If you ask a silly question, you've only got yourself to blame as somebody — shades of Empire! — once told a first-time buyer who enquired innocently if St George's Day was still commonly observed on building sites!)

The skeletal roof scantlings stood out rib-cage stark, for the flag had been flown for the best part of a week, the carpenters having followed hard on the heels of the brickies. So far, the hoped-for response from the customer had not materialised and there were suggestions from some of the men that, to get their own back, the chimney pots be slated over.

Meanwhile, zombie-like, Jake had been carrying out his tasks with minimal communion.

"If only he'd say 'Arsoles!' at least then we'd know he was still with us," grumbled one bricklayer, resigned to getting no more than a grunt or a shrug of the shoulders in response to enquiry after Jake's welfare, or invective regarding his current sub-standard work performance.

"'E's a millstone roun' our necks, a bleed'n' rod to our backs. I don't know why Lappitt don't pension him off," one of the older men complained.

"Hey you, Jake! Gerrup there and fix that bloody flag," commanded the foreman as he turned into the site office. He was used to being obeyed at the double.

Jake, squinting aloft, groaned, momentarily leaning against the scaffolding. A length of tile batten that had been doing flagpole duty had overnight snapped and now drooped drunkenly, its signal hidden from view.

Pulling himself together and muttering softly between his teeth, the labourer climbed the ladder with customary ease, then threaded his way through the rafters and over the ceiling joists to the chimney stack. Mission accomplished, he had retraced his steps almost to the scaffold when, relaxing slightly, he completely missed his footing, fell across the roof plate between rafters and flopped sideways on to the boards — fortunate that for once the toeboards were firmly in place, for he lunged against one of them with some force, saving him a twenty foot dive to terra firma, but dislocating a shoulder.

"I knowed 'e were gonna do summat daft, felt it in me bones," growled Andy, who was first on the scene. He was a large man, well-proportioned and strong as an ox. Without hesitation and assisted by one of the carpenters, he yanked Jake on to his feet and, making use of the jinny wheel rope, piggy-backed him down the ladder to the ground. Jake, shaken and in some pain, was still and quiet as they cradled him against a brick stack and sent an apprentice to alert the foreman.

When he visited the cottage hospital in the early evening, Lappitt, while pleased to learn from the ward sister that the patient was "comfortable", couldn't help but note how Jake's general condition had deteriorated since the stores incident. He was a pale shadow of his former self.

Swallowing hard, Sam looked anxiously down at the labourer, with some alarm recalling Parsley Jack's words: "You shouldn't have gone at him bald-headed. You know what a big softie he is! Why couldn't you 'ave just dealt with him gentle-like? — tell him he could've had a few nails anytime he wanted if only he'd ask for them". As a student of human nature, Jack was way ahead of his boss.

The fact that Jake was under sedation only made matters worse, for Sam panicked easily and, noting the patient's sickly pallor, very soon convinced himself it was all his fault.

Sitting by the bedside contemplating the motionless figure, he recalled how Jack had once said that Jake was "one in a thousand", that there was something special in his make-up that attracted people. Certainly, he wasn't the only one to have noticed that dogs and children especially perked up no end when he spoke to them. Yet, mused Sam, he was only a labourer, and one not quite right in the head at that.

Leaving the hospital, he called at the *Nag's Head*, fortifying himself with a double Scotch before heading reluctantly in the direction of Jake's house because he knew the least he could do was to slip a word of sympathy and encouragement to Mavis. He found her fixing up a bed in the front room against the possibility that, when her man came out of hospital, he might be unable to climb the stairs.

Sam sat at the kitchen table.

Mavis insisted on making a pot of tea and, as she fetched the sugar from the wall cabinet, Sam noted the way she gently tapped the side of the bowl with the palm of her hand to bring the granules into a tidy, rounded heap, a habit left over from years in service before her marriage. He was always on the lookout for little things like that; it filled in the gaps between the chit-chat, and he would deduce, usually accurately, the whys and the wherefores.

As she poured the tea she recounted the full story of how Jake came to take the nails. Sam was devastated. Never in his life had he felt so humbled, so hopelessly contrite.

A kindly woman, she could see he was affected and genuinely concerned about Jake. Despite her own troubles, she felt constrained to bolster up his spirits in the only way she knew how.

"Drink up your tea, Mr Lappitt, and I'll read your cup. I'm quite good at it really. I never use them tea bags."

Certainly she had quite a reputation in the neighbourhood for being able to summon up all sorts of fantasies from studying tea leaf dregs, and missed no opportunity to display her fortune telling skills.

Normally, he would have played along with the idea for, like most people, he was very curious about the foretelling of the future. But not now. He had other things on his mind. He was thoroughly miserable, and not in the mood for make-believe.

It was in this condition that he arrived home to be met in the hall by Mrs L, who had been stoking the fires of rancour since, fuming because he had not come in to time, she'd put his dinner in the oven.

"Where do you think you've been all this time? Supporting the bar at the *Nag's Head*, I suppose." Then, without pausing, ". . . and I don't for a minute expect you've done anything yet about Helen's roof?"

It was more than a man could stand. He should have stood his ground, but instead, without a word of explanation, retreated via the back kitchen and the yard to the carpenter's shop. As usual, this was his last refuge, the only certain sanctuary, for he knew *she* wouldn't dare put a foot inside, believing it to be rat-ridden and infested with outsize spiders.

He peeled off his jacket and threw himself down on a heap of wood shavings. Here, on his jack, he could reassess the cardinal virtues and weigh the current standing of the House of Lappitt.

When Mrs Hardcastle, Helen's mother-in-law, lowered her spare, arthritic frame into the recliner chair in her upstairs bed-sit after seeing to the lunchtime washing-up, she was angry with herself.

Secretly, she had a great admiration for her daughter-in-law, thought her a capable, well-mannered girl, gave her full marks for the way in which she managed her children and kept her irascibly-inclined husband under control. Nevertheless, she was forever nagging Helen about one thing or another — for constantly pandering to the cat in its pernickety feeding habits; displaying undue familiarity in her dealings with tradesmen; being too free with caramel wafers and chocolate biscuits when the children came home from school. She couldn't help being critical; it was second nature to her and the more she fought against it, the worse she got.

Now, she really was put out because she'd made a fool of herself. At lunch, she had been carrying on about the futility of depending on the likes of Lappitt for the roofing work. Shaking her head to emphasise her point, she prophesied that the job would never be done "if you have to rely on that man".

The words were scarcely out of her mouth when Lappitt's lorry drew up outside, tackle and material off-loaded, and the work commenced.

It was nearly a month since the night Mrs Lappitt, sitting in front of the applewood fire, introduced to her husband the subject of Helen's roof.

Since then, Sam had made every endeavour to shift the job on to a specialist firm, but when the quotes came in, he had to agree with Herbert that they were skyhigh; so much so that it was evident the flat roofing fraternity was currently flush with work and, consequently, not in the mood to entertain bread and butter stuff.

Jake had made a partial recovery and Lappitt, still full of remorse at his treatment of the labourer, and intent on atonement, went out of his way to ease him back to normal employment via as much light work as he could rustle up. Pushed into a corner by the roofing firms' negative interest, he'd reluctantly fallen back on the idea of getting all-rounder Quasimodo to do the job, with Jake as labourer.

From her comfortable chair, Mrs Hardcastle watched the men going up and down the ladder outside her window and listened to the tearing, scraping, bumping and thumping that went on above her head as the old felt was ripped off the roof and preparations made for renewal to the flat and the skirting round the half-brick parapet wall.

Once or twice she almost nodded off, but when eventually she did so, she was awakened almost immediately by several extra loud thuds which shook the room and set the pendant light dancing. Wide awake on the instant, raised voices alerted her to the fact that something untoward had happened.

At first, motionless, she stared straight in front of her and, uncomprehending, watched the window clouding over as a moving mass of black glutinous substance flowed smoothly down the panes and over the laybars, blotting out the sunshine. She opened her mouth to shout but no sound came, and it was a couple of minutes before she could summon up enough strength to get out of her chair and make tracks for the stairs.

By the time she found Helen, news of the catastrophe

had already spread, as had the black stuff.

If looking at it from the inside had been disturbing for Mrs Hardcastle, seen by Helen from the outside produced an even more shattering effect.

She was found by her mother-in-law standing in the garden, hands covering her face, peering tearfully at the house through her fingers as if to minimise the stark reality of the situation.

A wide, sticky band of bituminous matter coated brickwork and windows from top to bottom of the extension, and had begun to creep Quatermass-like through the herbaceous border under the laundry room window.

The two workmen, loathe to descend, and now powerless to intervene, stayed silent and apprehensive while studying their handiwork — riveted to the spot near the parapet wall lately breached by the five-gallon drum whose contents, having done its worst to the structure, now snaked over the garden path and lapped the lawn like a lava flow intent on maximal havoc.

At the moment when the two women came together, the only movement or sound issued from an astonished and angry tabby cat whose rear end was changing colour because, although alerted by the noise of the container crashing through the parapet, it had been oblivious to the approaching menace at its back as, squatting on the concrete path, it preened its whiskers with velvet paw. Between frantic attempts to dispose of the goo by claw and tongue, it voiced extreme displeasure, eventually streaking into the house through the open kitchen door.

This galvanised Helen into action as realisation dawned that the cat could spread the tar all over the house. After dealing with this situation she popped a water biscuit into her mouth to placate her peptic ulcer which, responding to the general alarm, had started a niggle.

Meanwhile, children on the way home from school collected outside the house, fascinated by the unusual spectacle and staring goggle-eyed. It was as if they had suddenly been presented with a great treat, watching events with close attention, voicing their pleasure with a deal of noise and interspersing humorous comments with fits of giggling.

When at last the two workers came gingerly down the ladder, there were gasps of admiration and excitement from the children as they observed at close quarters the extent of the men's discomfiture; they were plastered in treacly, glossy black tar almost from head to foot. The quiet, sedate avenue rang with peals of wicked laughter and cries of rapturous appreciation. It was better than Laurel and Hardy or the telly because it was real and was happening right here before their very eyes.

So far, the funny side of it had eluded Helen and Mrs Hardcastle. It was the latter who spoke first when the men appeared at the foot of the ladder.

"A fine mess you've made of it!" she reproached with some heat, puffed-up with restored justification of her lunchtime criticism of Lappitt management, yet dithering in her shoes at the dimension of the calamity that had befallen them.

"Leave it to me, mother," Helen interposed, quietly but firmly.

She had known Jake for many years and now, as she clapped eyes on him, her heart overflowed with compassion, all other emotion subsiding in the face of his pitiful condition. He had received the full treatment; face, arms and clothing were saturated when he slipped and fell full length in an abortive attempt to prevent the drum spilling out its entire contents.

On the other hand his mate, Quasimodo, hunchback kingpin of the blue-eyed bricklayers — so-called by mechanics at the lower end of the craft hierarchy resentful of Lappitt's preferential treatment — had got off comparatively lightly, except for his overalls which he quickly discarded.

Quasi was the first to respond. He had a good head for emergencies.

"We're truly sorry about this, ma'am. I can assure you it was not our fault — a couple of the boards were rotten and the canopy wall was frost damaged." Turning to Helen he continued, "If you will stay calm and give us a chance, we will put everything right, you'll see. Can we have all your old newspapers and as many rags as you can lay your hands on? If I can borrow your bike, I'll get off to the yard and see if I can find a solution to clean up the brickwork and arrange for the lorry to bring us the stuff to finish off."

Before long, Mrs Hardcastle, almost despite herself, was responding to the new situation. After all, she told herself, it *was* an emergency just like in the war, and they must all buckle-to and pull together.

"Butter!" she called out shrilly. "That's what we want — butter! It's just the thing for getting tar off the skin. That cheap common market stuff'll do. And Helen! go and see what turps and meths you've got."

The prospect of having something really worthwhile to do for a change, stimulated her. And the example of and taste for leadership was contagious; she would certainly stand in for Quasi while he was away at the yard. Cheeks flushed and mustering a remarkable burst of energy, she shuffled off to the garden shed to retrieve some of the old newspapers and magazines the family collected assiduously week after week for Shelter.

Helen and Jake knelt opposite one another on the lawn. She and her mother-in-law had helped him clean himself up, and he now sported an old pair of Herbert's flannel trousers; now, they were concentrating on the moggy which, surprisingly, after dashing all over the place like a whirling Dervish, had become quiet and compliant.

Helen was astonished at the ease with which Jake handled the animal.

"You've got the touch, haven't you Jake? He'd never let me handle him like that, not in these circumstances. Next time he's got canker, I'll know who to send for."

"It's nothin' really," Jake replied modestly, accepting the compliment. "Me mother used to say I could handle a wild bull."

"I bet you could, too," declared Helen with conviction.

Herbert was furious when he came home from his work and discovered what had happened. Though some of the mess had been cleared up, Jake and Quasi were still in the thick of it. Working their way down from the top, they had cleaned off most of the brickwork immediately under the flat roof, also part of the bedroom window frame and sash.

Quasi, prepared for conflict, made to descend the ladder when he became aware of the irate figure of Helen's husband hovering around and scowling up at him from below. But he needn't have bothered. Ignoring the two workmen, Herbert got back into his car where he had left it in the drive, and drove off at speed and in a manner which suggested both urgency and choler.

Sam was aware that something had gone wrong, because Quasi had said so. But what Quasi had not done was to enlighten him as to the extent of the misfortune that had overtaken them; in fact he had rather played it down on the basis that, come inspection time, the evidence would have been substantially removed.

So, when Herbert stormed into the yard and started to berate Sam for incompetence, dereliction of duty and criminal damage to property, the builder was almost entirely ignorant of the facts and, although taken aback by the verbal assault on the good name of his firm, for once did the right thing.

"Oh, go to hell!" he responded angrily and, shrugging off the censure, growled, "I didn't want your bloody job to start with. I'll have a look at it *after* I've had my tea," saying which he turned on his heel, marched off in the direction of his quarters, and left Herbert standing there hardly able to contain his rage.

Quasi and Jake worked right through to the early evening, fortified by cups of tea and sandwiches supplied by the attentive Mrs Hardcastle, who had enthusiastically joined with Helen in making the best of things. Due in no small measure to Helen's considerate attitude and encouragement, Jake had made a surprisingly good recovery from the shock of his unfortunate fall on the flat roof and, not being used to having a fuss made of him, was quite happy until Herbert, mooching around to see what else he could find to criticise, blew his top when he spotted the labourer wearing his "favourite pair of slacks" — as he described them — annoyed that Helen should pass them on without his permission.

Just then, Sam appeared, girding his loins. Herbert seized on him.

"Just look at this, Lappitt! Have you ever seen such a debacle in all your life? How would you feel if you came home after a hard day's work to find your house vandalised and . . . and a bloody workman wearing your favourite pants?"

Sam was not only surprised, but appalled at what he saw. He remained silent, taking it all in, mad at Quasi for leading him up the garden, and beginning to doubt the wisdom of his decision to employ Jake on such a job. As he surveyed the mess he had to admit it was the worst day's work in the history of the firm, and he could well understand how Herbert had come to mount his high horse.

However, before he could respond, Quasi intervened. He had a fine flair for putting his oar in to back up his boss in arguments with clients — incidental to extricating himself from awkward situations. Adopting a quizzical stance, he enquired, "Am I right, Mr Lappitt,. in believing that you accepted this job on the understanding that we use that new-type blackjack?"

"That's right," assured Sam, almost absent-mindedly, still shaken by the sight of the black stuff plastered over the brickwork and windows.

"Well," suggested Quasi, now addressing Herbert, "we'd have been in a right old mess if it had been red hot pitch, wouldn't we? First degree burns, hospital, insurance problems, claims for damages and all the rest of it!"

"Yes," responded Sam, perking up, "that's right enough! Herbert! *you* have a lot to be thankful for!"

Herbert stared in disbelief. Suddenly, the case was altered; now, he had to thank his lucky stars it wasn't worse. He didn't like it.

It wasn't the first time Quasi had displayed a knack for showing Sam the way ahead. Now the boss knew what he had to do.

"Quasi! Jake! Jack it in *now*. What's left can wait till the morning. Might be easier to deal with when it's hard, anyway."

He looked boldly at Herbert and, as once again he recalled the insults fired at him in the yard, his attitude hardened.

"Next time you want anything done, you can find somebody else."

There was a time when many of Pickstock's pub and beerhouse landlords eked out but a sparse living, finding it necessary to supplement their incomes by working part-time in the chair factories down river. Not so Nick McShane, of the *Nag's Head*; he was thriving when most of the others were struggling, and over a longish period established himself in the community as a man of substance and authority.

He was not behindhand in having his say or being critical of those who used his premises, be they town councillors, businessmen or public bar regulars. Some said he'd got too big for his boots, while others argued there was nothing like a bit of gossip or candid comment to keep the atmosphere alive; and there was no denying that if it was a quiet drink you wanted, there were plenty of places around where you'd get precious little else.

It might be thought that Jake's convalescence would have suffered a setback as a result of the flat roof mishap, but not a bit of it. If she did nothing else, Helen had illustrated by her positive reaction, how a situation could be upended and turned to some account; and Mavis recognised that, far from being a setback, it had been a turning point in Jake's return to what for him passed for normality.

The understanding and charity Helen had displayed to both Quasi and Jake had, considering the circumstances, gone a long way to restore their faith in human nature.

Jake was soon ready to revert to his usual leisure time habits — taking a drink at the weekends and having a game of shove ha'penny in the *Nag's Head* with the best of them.

McShane had missed Jake's custom for some time, assuming that for one reason or another he had defected to the *Cherry Tree*. So, when he reappeared, far from being pleased the landlord passed sarcastic remarks about some folks' idea of loyalty to their locals and funny ways of showing appreciation of past favours gladly given. All this was way above Jake's head; he had no idea what the man was on about or why he hadn't been welcomed back with open arms and a drink on the house.

When one of Thomson's men came into the bar and blew the gaffe about Jake's involvement in Lappitt's flat roofing fiasco, general hilarity ensued in which McShane joined with gusto.

"Anybody 'ere want their 'ouse tarred?" he enquired, mimicking Lappitt and looking searchingly around the room. "Sam Lappitt's got a li'le ol' gang wot specialises in this kind of work, free estimates and satisfaction guaranteed. Ain't that right, Jake?" he added with mock solemnity, turning to face him as the merriment continued unabated.

If at that moment Jake had had any beer left in his pot he would have let McShane have it full in the face. As it was, without response, he rose and walked out of the pub, the landlord calling after him persuasively, "Aw, don't be like that, Jake!"

The moment the door swung shut behind him, Jake exploded. He broke into a trot, then ran full pelt down the middle of the high street, face flushed with anger, the sound of the bar room laughter ringing in his ears.

"I'll show yer, ye buggers, I'l show yer," he called out to all and sundry.

Ten minutes later he was back at the *Nag's Head*, a voluminous black dustbin liner slung over his shoulder.

Entering the pub, in one movement he heaved the heavy plastic bag on to the bar counter and slit it open from top to bottom with a deft flick of the penknife held ready to hand.

Sudden and complete silence pervaded the room as the spellbound customers watched the contents of the bag — fish heads, guts, entrails and other putrefying fishmongers' filth — ooze and slither all over the bar and on to the floor on either side. McShane, mesmerised, looked helplessly on as the slimy stream lapped his feet and slid through the open cellar flap from which he had just emerged.

The stench was overpowering. Drinking, shove ha'penny, darts, all bar activity ceased instantly. For once McShane was speechless as customers from other parts of the pub, becoming aware that something was afoot, filed in to stand and stare.

Satisfied that he had made his point, Jake carefully replaced the penknife in his pocket and quietly took himself off, pausing at the door to turn and grin affably at the assembled company.

There were customers who reckoned McShane was never the same man again; that, in fact, the incident not only knocked all the stuffing out of him, but caused him to go into a decline. It was one thing having to knuckle under to some smart alec customer, but quite another to be bested by a big softie like Jake. Within a twelvemonth he retired.

Jake, on the other hand, went from strength to strength. Men who hitherto had thought of him only as being soft in the head, now patted him on the back and told him what a great fellow he was. Not since Nipper Barton got into the ABC flyweight finals at Wembley had they been so enthusiastic about the achievement of a fellow townsman.

The labourer took it all quite calmly. He took his pint as well, regularly, and enjoyed a game of shove ha'penny at the *Cherry Tree*. And whenever he trotted down the street feinting and dribbling with a tin can at his feet, the founding fathers, shading themselves under the plane trees, would nod and smile indulgently, well content that Jake had done himself credit and put McShane in his place.

Mister Nightingale

WHEALER held his spectacles under the kitchen tap, letting the water flush over the lenses while rubbing them carefully between finger and thumb. It was a habit acquired from his old mother who went through the same rigmarole daily, pooh-pooing a neighbour's prediction that the metal-rimmed frames would rust and fall apart.

He replaced the glasses on his nose after wiping them on a roller towel fixed to the inside of the back door, then thoughtfully considered the morose countenance of the carpenter who, waiting for his tea to cool, sat at the table tinkering with the sugar bowl.

"*Everything's* an effort, Peter, be it chopping logs, going to work or even making love, but there is no doubt it is because of our rooted indolence that some of us fail in the long term."

The carpenter frowned and shuffled his feet uncomfortably under the table. He knew only too well what the boss was getting at.

"Look at it from my point of view," the builder continued, emphatically, "the work you've done in our back bedroom — rebuilding the fitted wardrobe, renewing the skirtings, repairing the flooring and the rest — why, if I was to charge a customer half what that's cost in labour he would play hell, and rightly so."

For years Whealer's mother had been at him to have these repairs and alterations done, and at long last he had grudgingly spared a carpenter to carry out the work.

Watching Peter's sugar doodling, he went on, "I well remember your dad — dear old Dicky Gale, bless him! — coming to me all those years ago saying he wanted his lad to be a carpenter; and, right enough, you became a first-rate tradesman. But the time you've taken on this job! I have to say it, Peter, it's not economical."

He waited for a response which, however, was not forthcoming.

"I don't know what's got into you, because I know you can do it. . . ."

Whealer's widowed mother came in and proceeded to fuss about at the stove where she was steaming a bit of haddock for her son's tea. She liked the carpenter and her interruption was timely, or so she thought, for she knew very well what was afoot.

"Would you care for another cup, Peter? Or a chocolate biscuit?" Her voice was friendly, compensatory.

"No thank you, Mrs Whealer."

"Oh, go on, have a chocolate biscuit," she coaxed. "There's plenty here." She reached for a coloured tin from the top of the fridge and proffered it.

"No thank you."

She put the tin on the table.

"Just leave us, mother, will you." There was a testy edge to the builder's voice.

Obediently, the old lady left the kitchen.

The telephone rang in the hall. Obeying the summons Whealer turned towards the door, at the same time addressing the carpenter in a surprisingly conciliatory manner.

"Anyway, take your time and finish your tea, Peter. I'll see you at the yard in the morning. I've an interesting little job I want you to have a look at. . . ."

Peter, patently unexcited at this prospect, drained his cup.

". . . Charlie's at Brookside and, as you know, the two apprentices are on the council site. You can have the run of the carpenter's shop."

As soon as the door closed, Peter quickly poured himself another cup of tea and, taking a chocolate biscuit from the tin, thoughtfully nibbled it round the edge.

It was all right for Whealer, he mused; he had everything going for him and nothing to worry about, certainly not a nagging wife.

Peter had been in the wars of late. He'd had one row after another with his wife, Agnes, principally because he wouldn't agree to apply for one of the new council houses being built at the east end of the town, she arguing it was time they moved from their cramped quarters — a two-up, two-down, turn of the century terraced cottage — so that their family could stretch itself a bit. But he was stubborn. He liked their little home and couldn't bear to think of moving to council property.

Another thing that rankled with her was the time he spent at the cottage hospital. Several times a week he'd call there in the evenings, chatting up the inmates and showing an interest and compassion which lately had been entirely absent from his relationship with wife or workmates.

The habit started when Sam, their next door neighbour — aged, widowed and worn out — had been taken there to die; which he promptly did. Peter had continued his visiting, however, encouraged by the nursing staff for his helpfulness and welcomed by the patients for his companionship.

Now, to cap it all, there was this new problem to contend with; his eyesight. It was worrying. He knew very well he should have had his eyes tested long ago, and especially since he'd noticed the quickening deterioration.

Hearing Whealer noisily replace the telephone on the hall table, and having no wish to encourage him to renew the grilling, Peter quickly grabbed his tool grip and skipped smartly out of the back door.

The talk in the shed was about anti-burglar devices, window catches, deadlocks and other deterrents required to be fitted to an exacting specification by the architect of the so-called executive type houses on which the gang was working.

An ancient, cast-iron combustion stove standing on a concrete plinth in the centre of the dirt floor wafted and belched its fumes at the surrounding company. Loaded to capacity with timber off-cuts and coke, it roared and crackled as though threatening to explode at any moment. Nobody took any notice. It was alive, warm and familiar.

"The folk 'avin' them 'ouses is bloomin' lucky the architect does take precautions," Danny reckoned. "When you're well-off you *would* get worried about your stuff gettin' nicked, wouldn't ya?"

"Waste of time," said Arch. Then, brows knitting, "but where does all the money come from? — that's what I'd like to know."

"I could do wi' some on it," Des ventured, thoughtfully. "When I was in the Ox and Jocks, there was this posh officer — Jumbo, they called him. . . ."

Without ceremony, Albert brushed aside this attempt to deviate and muscle-in on the chit-chat. (Des needed no encouragement to natter on about army life.)

"Where does the money come from?" he sneered loudly. "Why! it's them stockbrokers and financiers wot cultivates and farms it. Grows on trees in the City, don't it? And any time you walks up the high street you can see it staring at you from the estate agents' winders. We're the mugs — the bricks and mortar brigade. My old chap's right: nobody never made money, real money, by hard work."

The men sat around taking it all in while munching their bread and cheese, chattering and interrupting Westminster fashion as the spirit moved, but coming together with sudden shout and garbled comment when a point was made that tickled their fancy or ran counter to accepted shed wisdom.

Following Albert's contribution, Charlie — he had lately been seconded to the site from the yard temporarily to accelerate carpentry second fixings — seized the opportunity to sharpen his saw and harangue the brethren.

"*We* are the fortunates! We, who are nobodies, come here to eat our bait, drink, talk, joke; sometimes even to think aloud on life's pains and death's releases. We are the lucky ones. *We* have no use for burglar alarms or security locks and the rest of it, being without estate and so having bugger-all to pinch. *We* have nothing a-plenty — but, as The Man says, we will inherit the earth."

Carried away by this vision of the aristocracy of the poor, Charlie, hand raised as though in benediction, declaimed theatrically, "Oh, happy happy condition! Blessed are the chosen!"

"Gerroff, ya daft sod!" jeered Nick, the plumber.

Some of the men laughed, some were bemused; nevertheless, all relished the carpenter's antics,

Nobody believed they would inherit the earth, but Charlie's rhetoric boosted the corporate ego, gave a fillip to self-esteem, and momentarily bonded the social union of work and circumstance.

Charlie turned to his neighbour and whacked him heartily between the shoulder blades.

"Tom," he said, "you should get down on your hands and knees and thank God that he made you a have-not, a simple common man with only basic needs, uncomplicated by ambition and the lust for gold, content to propagate the species and top-up nightly with Wethereds best bitter."

There was a sudden clatter of corrugated iron

sheeting as the wind got up outside; and a scraping of feet as old Gus, the teaboy, replenished some of the mugs from the tea bucket which, balanced precariously on top of the stove, sizzled and leaked its contents into the ashcan.

Albert appeared puzzled.

"I thought the meek was to inherit the earth?"

"All right, so it's the meek," agreed Charlie reluctantly. "How much meeker can you get; if you've nothing in your pocket, yer gonna be awful meek, aren't you?"

He was generally well-liked by his mates, who admired him because, although he graduated from grammar school with flying colours he had, against all expectation and advice, stuck to a boyhood ambition to become a carpenter and joiner. Above all else, however, the men liked a chap who had the gift of the gab, and in this respect Charlie was well equipped.

Tom, who was known to have sired at least nine children in and out of wedlock, was seen to be deep in thought. Slowly, as though the point had only just percolated the cerebral lobes, he came out with, "'Ere, 'ang on, cleverdick! When did you last see me tipplin' Wethereds? I'm a Brakespeare man, I am. An' who says I ain't got no ambition?"

Tow-headed Albert, a big man with a forceful voice which often gave his commonplace opinions added weight, piped up, "That's right! Depends what you mean by ambition, don't it? An' what's this about lust? Our Tom's got bags o' lust, more so than most folk in Pickstock. Ain't you, Tom?"

Tom seemed almost abashed by this invasion of his privacy for, like most ladies men, he kept a tight lip on his affairs; the chaps who had the most to say on the subject were generally those with the least practical experience. However, Alf stepped into the breach.

"And what's more, Tom's got proof galore."

"Yeh," agreed Frank, "not like Ed here and the rest o' them young uns who tells us all about their conquests, but got nothin' to show for it; they could be bloomin' virgins for all we know. We've only got their word for it, after all, ain't we?"

"Too true," exclaimed Charlie. "Time was when you could easily tell who'd been on active service."

"I could never see nothin' in them French letters," quavered teaboy Gus, in his day an avid bird fancier.

"I was a bugger for the women when I was young," claimed Albert, with more than a touch of pride in his voice.

Of course, everyone in the gang knew it had been his younger brother, Tim (now a swashbuckling sub-contract bricklayer working in Reading), who was the womaniser, the one who, even as a lad, dared to scandalise — like pouring treacle over Snoddy's sweet-shop window after the owner boxed his ears when he discovered him pinching the liquorice all-sorts; or skinning alive old Paddy Brien's ginger tom when he came across it spraying and tending the calls of nature in his dad's cabbage patch. Tim, without doubt, was the black sheep of that family.

It was remarkable how Albert and his like wanted to be known as the black sheep of the family, though not necessarily to *be* the black sheep: just to borrow that special aura, that devil-may-care flamboyance that rightly belonged to another.

There was an element of the same genre apparent when a workmate stole something, resulting in a great hue and cry. Everyone would know who the culprit was, but no-one would let on, and it was not only because of fear of getting involved. They felt there was a narrowness, an austerity, a dryness about total honesty which was unattractive. A little soft brush with

Satan couldn't be all bad, could it? when it raced the blood, flushed the cheeks and caused the same tingling sensation as a cat must get when it raids the kitchen table.

So, Albert was not the only one who, on occasion, laid claim to a risque reputation.

He also liked to be looked upon as something of a tippler. Once, when he fell out with Charlie over the best way to set about cutting a complicated architect-designed roof, the latter told him disparagingly he should be thankful that a weak stomach and an ugly phisog had saved him from a life of drunkenness and fornication. He tended to look down his nose at Albert, whom he labelled as "nowt but a bodger".

However, Albert did have one redeeming feature. He never bore a grudge; though, here again, some said that only proved how shallow he was.

When the badinage triggered by the carpenter's boasting had subsided, Des said, regarding ambition, "I does me Littlewoods, don't I?"

"Yeh," Albert answered, "but they blokes wot's 'avin them 'ouses don't do no Littlewoods. They 'ave their own kind of Littlewoods, an' you can bet your bottom dollar the odds ain't a million to one against them collectin' *their* divis."

"Mind the time Pete won the pools?" someone called out.

This produced a deal of raucous laughter and a chant of "Money to burn, money to burn".

Convinced he had won a substantial sum and urged on by his workmates, Peter had invested the whole of his savings — almost twenty pounds — in a nosh-up at the *Wheatsheaf* on the Monday evening. It was a great "do" and appreciated by all, but when the news got around that never before had so many pollsters won so little on any one Saturday afternoon, Peter realised too late that he had jumped the gun and landed in the soup with Agnes.

Even when he handed over the pools cheque, instead of showing appreciation she screwed it up and contemptuously threw it on the fire — considering the grand gesture well worth it for, as she remarked, what could you buy for three quid that you couldn't get out of any Friday's pay packet?

So, for years to come, she got her dividends regularly in the re-telling of the oft-told tale.

"Have you heard about Pete," Frank enquired of Albert.

"Heard what? Been working at the yard, ain't 'e — doin' summat to Spokey's bedroom?"

"I don't reckon he'll be working much longer at the yard, or anywhere else. He's going blind."

"No! Who told you that?"

"My missus. She sees Agnes at the townswomens' guild and she says Pete's bin going down the nick ever since he fell off his bike one day in the Spring coming back from the allotment. 'E can barely see to read the paper. 'Ow 'e does 'is job, I'm blowed if I knows. Wonder 'e don't do 'isel' a mischief."

"I can hardly believe that. Bit sudden, ain't it?"

"Bin comin' on for a long time."

"Does Whealer know?"

"If 'e don't, 'e soon will."

Charlie, who had been out of earshot when Frank was retailing the news about Peter, was now intent on stirring it up and, returning to the original discussion regarding the executive type house buyers, remonstrated persuasively, "Personally, I feel more sympathy than envy for these chaps. They are burdened with possessions, eaten up with anxiety, apprehensive at every knock on the door afeared that the tax man cometh. Have you never thought of it that way? Does it not give you a lump in the throat to think how much of an uphill struggle it is for your fellow men to protect their property?"

The gang's expression of ridicule at this foolery quickly evaporated when the door of the shed was unceremoniously thrown open and the foreman, waving his arms about, told them to "Get up off them rumps: you're twenty minutes into Whealer time. . . ."

"Aw, 'ave an 'eart, guv. . . . We was late comin' in. . . ."

"Out, out, out!" ordered the foreman, in no mood to parley.

For the moment at least, Peter was content, almost replete, at rest with the world.

Earlier in the evening he had called at the cottage hospital and done the rounds; animating, chivvying, cheering, and fetching and carrying for the old dears who had become the focus of his nursing care. Short staffed as usual, the sister and her part-timers welcomed any help they could get from volunteers, in particular to stimulate and interest their charges to what was going on in the community at large.

For him, no task was too menial, no patient too far gone to merit his full and careful attention. As soon as he stepped inside the precincts he was a new man; keen, eager to please and displaying charity and kindliness in abundance. He concentrated on a mixed bag of decrepit Pickstock folk in their declining years, generally referred to as geriatrics, though few in fact were entirely in that category.

For instance, there was blind, 94-year-old Sukey who would engage him to read aloud snippets from the local paper, and adjust and fit new batteries to her hearing aid; Sidney, whose weak bladder and unreliable bowel kept him continually on the trot, had been pattern maker and pigeon fancier before moving in with his daughter — he would lie in wait to buttonhole for a "crack" anyone who happened by, besides soliciting a short back and sides or help with his pools; superior Miss Charlotte who might be out of the local top drawer (and made sure everyone knew it), but, nevertheless, had something of the same needs as the rest, such as nails to be cut and, because of failing eyesight, private mail to be deciphered and replies penned and posted; and Jack Evans, retired bricklayer, whose requirements were few, but who enjoyed nothing better than to reminisce about building trade artisans of a bygone age employed by local firms, some long since defunct — and so on. . . .

As always when he'd completed his self-imposed stint, Peter felt pleased with himself, satisfied that there were at least some folk who benefited by contact with him. That, he considered, was return enough for services rendered.

From this, you might think he was now at home, comfortably ensconced in his favourite chair by the kitchenor stove and listening to the nine o'clock news on the wireless, as was his wont.

Not so.

He was in fact lying full length on a pile of wood shavings in the carpenter's shop, smoking one of his favourite Woodbines and occasionally feeding his face from a bag of salted peanuts. The partly-eaten heel of a small wholemeal loaf lay on the floor on a copy of the *Daily Mirror*, alongside a half-empty tin of baked beans and a carton of milk.

No doubt about it, thought he, a great place was the carpenter's shop, bungful of atmosphere; a place for thinking through life's problems in a relaxed and civilised way while taking in the familiar aroma of wood shavings, sawdust and newly prepared Perana pine.

And no-one to argue with or say you nay!

Woodbine adrool, he stretched out on a pile of shavings

Utility-built when Queen Victoria was in her heyday, the outwardly unremarkable red brick edifice at the far end of the yard had housed succeeding generations of joiners, most of whom had spent the whole of their working lives within its confines.

Here, the currency of craft circulated like money in the bank, giving a first-rate man his dues in respect and esteem relative to those of lesser coin.

The most scholarly, however, was seldom the best tradesman. Charlie, normally in command of the shop and excellent craftsman though he was, could not hold a candle to Alf who was barely able to write his name, though he could read a plan well enough. Then again, when the firm ran a team in the local darts league, Whealer himself had to play second fiddle to Ding Dong, a brickie's labourer who could knock spots off his boss when it came to mental arithmetic, causing the latter to decline to "take chalks" rather than display his obvious mathematical inferiority.

As Peter stared upwards, noting the bits and pieces of discarded joinery stacked above the ceiling joists ("They'll come in handy some day", Whealer would say when stock-taking), he lit another Woodbine and let slip a contented sigh. This was the life. . . .

Meanwhile, not fifty yards away, in his dining room at the back of the office, Whealer finished supper, scraped back his chair on the parquet floor, and strolled into the yard to take a breather before rounding off the day by working out the lorry details for the morrow.

Several times a week he would saunter round the yard of an evening ruminating on the day's tribulations, assessing this, cursing that, teasing away at the pros and cons. Of late he had been critical of his own handling of the business and worried that he was not making the most of its potential. He knew very well that in some respects his approach to developing trends and expansion was not good enough, much too tentative.

In his time he had many opportunities to graduate to greater things, chances he let slip — like when he funked the new factory jobs at Slough after the war, which, as he suspected and time proved, provided many builders with repeat contracts employing umpteen men over a span of years; or work for the Church Commissioners or British Rail which, again, would have given top craft employment for as long as he wanted.

It wasn't as though he was short of the right sort of men. Over the years they'd tackled good class work — churches and factories, prestige offices and fantoosh flats; he had some of the best craftsmen in the South of England, and was adept at paying them just the right amount above the rate to keep them happy. And he was better than most of his contemporaries at pricing a bill of quantities or spot estimating smaller jobs on the right side.

Yet it seemed that at the critical moment he suffered a blockage, as though the prospect of stepping up the ladder brought on a kind of commercial vertigo which over-faced him; like a pools winner out of his depth or a navvy who couldn't hold his ale.

Ambition welled up just as it did with other men, but it was short lived, soon petered out, leaving him back-sliding into the soft option. Complete confidence in his own ability, but no stomach for the big time.

He was too much of a sentimentalist to be a go-getter or a potential captain of industry, was addicted to doing everything himself even when he had men well capable of doing it for him. And he was too interested in and concerned for the individual; perhaps because as a confirmed bachelor he had nothing better to think about.

His unease about Peter had grown daily. For some time he had watched his work deteriorate, and became convinced that idleness by itself was not the root cause.

As he listened and watched a song thrush perched high on the ridge of the carpenter's shop, he fancied he saw a light flicker in one of the top windows. Deciding to investigate, he climbed the outside stair and, finding the rickety double doors slightly ajar, shouldered his way into the shop, taking Peter completely unawares and scaring the daylights out of him as he lay spread-eagled among the shavings.

They stared at one another.

As the carpenter, in slow motion, removed the Woodbine from his mouth, Whealer, stunned and speechless, shifted his gaze and weighed up the situation.

He proceeded to prowl around the massive antique bench which dominated the centre of the shop.

Suddenly, he wheeled on Peter who was at last making a move to get up off the floor.

"I want a straight answer to a straight question: you bin campin' out, haven't you?"

Peter knew it was no good beating about the bush.

"Yes, Mr Whealer."

"Good god! Not all week, surely?"

"Yes, Mr Whealer."

The boss resumed his pacing up and down, fuming. From the bench he snatched up a large pub ashtray full to overflowing with Woodbine nubs, and shook it in front of Peter's nose.

"Did it never occur to you that one careless flick of the wrist could've set the whole place alight? With these shavings and this tinder dry timber it could've been an inferno in two minutes flat — out of control, a death-trap, with you in the middle roasted to a frazzle.

"And the insurance people! *They* would've stumped up without a murmur: I don't think!"

Peter stubbed his Woodbine in the ashtray which was now back on the bench.

"I have to question your sanity, Peter. What in hell's name's gotten into you?"

He pointed in the direction of the timber rack, adjoining which was a large "No Smoking" sign pinned to the top of the notice board which displayed the Factory Act Regulations.

"You know you're not supposed to smoke in here! What do you think that bloody notice means?" Whealer looked Peter sharply in the eye. "What is the matter with you? Are you sickening for something? I suppose you've fallen out with Agnes. Is that it?"

After waiting a moment for a reply, he continued, "Have you got nothing to say for yourself at all?"

Over the years Peter had observed that in altercation it was as well to let the other fellow talk himself to a standstill; like a yachtsman waiting for a gale to blow itself out. Certainly, he considered that if he held on long enough the other chap would at least change gear.

"Agnes's got it into her head she wants to move into one of them new council houses being built at the east end. Our cottage was condemned years ago."

"Ah! So you've fallen out! You should've gone into the spare room instead of shacking up here."

"I was packing up in the morning, anyway. She threatened to spill the beans on me, let you know what I was up to."

Again, Whealer paraded round the bench.

"You know very well you're supposed to leave the key on the board in the front office on your way out — not pocket it!"

Still incensed, he pointed to a bundle of sundry items of clothing and a rolled-up sleeping bag, and speaking slowly and distinctly concluded, "I want you to pick up your traps now, go home to Agnes and come and see me first thing Monday morning. . . ."

He strode across the shop, pausing as he was about to

go out of the door.

". . . and you can take that brewery ashtray and your fag ends with you."

When any of his employees, past or present, were admitted to the cottage hospital, Whealer would call to see them on a Sunday afternoon. It was almost a ritual with him. Pickstock born and bred, he was acquainted with most people in the town and, although he found small talk exceedingly painful — an abomination to the spirit — he would nevertheless chinwag sociably when occasion demanded. He was a good listener.

Jack Evans, the bricklayer, had suffered a stroke down his left side, but there were signs of a steady recovery.

He was pleased to see his ex-boss, but after a while the latter, tiring of Jack's tales of personality clashes and derring-do's on the building site, disengaged as tactfully as possible and went to seek out Sukey, lifelong friend and sometime neighbour of his mother.

She was a first class woman who, early on in life, found herself saddled with a third-rate husband, a ne'er-do-well; feckless, idle, he would have been a poor match for a strumpet. However, as sometimes happens in these circumstances, his defects were the making of her, she realising that to get anywhere at all would depend entirely on the exercise of her own initiative. Endowed with a good generator, she succeeded in keeping hearth and home together, employing her spare energies in community interests. But that was long, long ago. . . .

Whealer found the old lady sitting slumped in a chair by the side of her bed in the geriatric ward, blood bags under her watering eyes, sore and swollen legs bandaged from knee to ankle, and outstretched hand gripping a rolled-up flannel because she was unable to straighten out her arthritic joints.

For the umpteenth time, the modulator in her deaf aid bleeped and squealed for attention.

The hothouse atmosphere was stifling, and although strong antiseptic did its best to submerge the all-pervading smell of urine, it was a losing battle.

Some would say that society would not let a dog suffer like that old woman, and yet . . . and yet. . . . Sukey's bright, clear mind flashed and sparkled within its yellowed, well-nigh hairless cranium, and its miscellany of fact and feeling would certainly have stayed the hand of any mercy killer.

Whealer deftly adjusted the deaf aid and Sukey nodded her thanks; he was quite used to doing this, his mother being similarly afflicted.

"I can't grumble," was Sukey's reply to his enquiry and, blind eyes welcoming, hands touching, "I'm so glad you came to see me.

"I wanted a word with you about Peter, that carpenter of yours — Dick Gale's son — the one we call Mister Nightingale."

"Peter? Mr Nightingale? How d'ye mean?"

"You surely must have heard about Peter! He visits us old crocks several nights a week, makes himself useful and keeps us informed about you lot out there."

"Well, I'll be blowed! Fancy that!" Whealer was more than surprised, though he had difficulty focusing mentally on Peter, the Good Samaritan.

"He's an angel. Sister calls him her Number One."

"You do surprise me. My rating of Mister Nightingale will need some adjustment."

"Did you know he had a sight problem?"

"So that's it! I thought there must be something; I should have guessed." Patently, Whealer was vexed he had not probed further that evening in the carpenter's shop.

"I noticed recently," Sukey continued, "he'd been

avoiding reading me bits out of the *Courier*. Eventually it came out; he couldn't see. If nothing's done, you'll be minus a carpenter before very long. Not only that, his wife's been giving him a rough time, though I think she is in the right; pokey little holes those cottages in the King's Road, most unsuitable for bringing up a brood." Leaning towards him, she persuaded, "Could you not do something for them, Bobby?"

Her use of his mother's pet name for him — only she ever referred to him as "Bobby" — took him aback. He could only splutter and make sympathetic noises.

"Anyway, I'll finish my say. Sister reckons he's got cataracts, probably through taking steroids when he was asthmatic; it's not always just an old body's complaint. It's not a lost cause, but he should see a doctor right away."

Whealer noted the parchment-like skin hanging loose on bony arms, thin wisps of hair straggling across wet, highly coloured cheeks. As they age, thought he, some old folk shift out of focus with life, awareness blunted. Not Sukey.

"All right," he said, "you've had your say about Peter. I came here to enquire about *your* health and temper; my mother will be asking about you when I get back. How are you managing?"

"Oh, I'm all right. When you get to my age you tend to accept things as they are, not as you might like them to be; perhaps it's to prepare you for transfer to whatever comes next. You have to make your peace and accept that there are things you can't change — then 'go quietly'. But, coming back to Peter. . . ."

She was incorrigible, tenacious, single-minded.

So it came about that when Peter presented himself at the office in fear and trembling on the Monday morning, the situation developed quite differently to what he expected.

"You're to go to the surgery and see Dr O'Shea. I've spoken to him. He will be making an appointment for you to attend the eye clinic. Whatever you do, don't worry about it, Peter. You'll be a new man in a month. And another thing. We've got an odd little bit of ground in Mill Lane that I'd planned for a pair of small spec. houses. One of these I'm going to sell to you, if you'll have it. It won't be at any bargain price, but I'll see that you get the right deductions for the work you're going to do yourself in your spare time after you come out of hospital.

"You can do joists, roof, carpentry first and second fixings, decorations, and anything else you can handle; perhaps one of your mates could lend a hand. . . .

". . . Oh, and I'll see you get fixed up with a mortgage."

Peter could only stand and stare and mumble. Overcome by the turn of events, he could not have been more tongue-tied had he been given the sack.

"Off you go now," ordered Whealer. "By the time you've had the cataracts done, we'll be scaffold high on the pair, and you can order the joists . . . and mind you make a good job of it!"